She made him want things he had no business wanting...

Tony stroked the backs of his fingers across Hayden's soft cheek. So smooth. So tantalizing. Then he fisted her hair around his hands, the tendrils curling and tickling his skin. Hayden pressed herself against him, the oh-so-slight brush of her nipples against his chest making him crazy.

More.

Had she moaned that? Had he? Hell, yes, he wanted more. So much more. Everything.

But with a deep sigh, she put some distance between them and slumped against the seat of the car, fighting for breath.

He found it difficult to drag in air, too. He wrapped his fingers around the steering wheel, commanding his body to settle. But despite the pain he knew he'd be feeling on the drive back to Dallas, he had to chuckle.

"Guess that answers the question I asked earlier."

"What?" she said, her voice tight.

"You feel it, too..."

Dear Reader,

The idea for *Naked Thrill* came about on a crazy, GPS-failing car trip with my best friend. So of course, Hayden and Tony had to have one mind-blowing adventure, too.

My favorite kind of trips are when you just hop in the car with no plans and no reservations and just drive, only stopping when something catches your eye—you never know where this type of trip will lead you. Although I've never had a vacation where I've lost my memories or my clothes (yet), it was a blast starting off Hayden and Tony's journey that way and giving them an adventure neither could forget!

I'd like to say I felt a little guilty about making their lives so difficult, but I had too much fun seeing just how bad I could make it! I hope you enjoy reading about the detective work these two have to do on their past twenty-four hours, but also how they examine the choices and happenstances that put them on the path to finding one another.

You can always find me at my website, jillmonroe.com. Feel free to drop by unannounced!

Best,

Jill

Jill Monroe

Naked Thrill

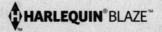

HARLEQUIN® BLAZE™

Recycling programs
for this product may
not exist in your area.

ISBN-13: 978-0-373-79869-8

Naked Thrill

Printed in U.S.A.

Jill Monroe makes her home in Oklahoma with her family. When not writing, she spends way too much time on the internet completing "research" or updating her blog. Even when writing, she's thinking of ways to avoid cooking.

Books by Jill Monroe

HARLEQUIN BLAZE

Share the Darkness
Hitting the Mark
Tall, Dark and Filthy Rich
Primal Instincts
Wet and Wild
SEALed and Delivered
SEALed with a Kiss

HARLEQUIN NOCTURNE

Lord of Rage

To get the inside scoop on Harlequin Blaze and its talented writers, be sure to check out BlazeAuthors.com.

All backlist available in ebook format.

Visit the Author Profile page at Harlequin.com for more titles.

This book is dedicated to my family, who, let's face it, put up with a lot!

Special thanks to Gena Showalter—I thought about listing all the crazy places and misadventures we've had together, but, you know, NDA!

Special thanks to Deidre Knight and Adrienne Macintosh—you ladies are great!

1

HAYDEN STRETCHED LAZILY beneath the softness of the silk sheet. Ahhhh, heaven. Nothing like sleeping in late, allowing the chirping of the birds and the warmth of the sun on her cheek to wake her. She'd never been so warm.

Wait a minute. She didn't have silk sheets. And the kind of warmth next to her could only be provided by—oh, no.

Hayden's eyes popped open. Well, as much as her worn-out body would allow her eyes to pop after doing who knows what the night before. Every muscle ached and her lips were dry from—uh-huh, probably from too much lip-lock. Her fingers bunched into the sheet at her chest.

Please don't be naked. Please don't be naked.

She raised the sheet.

One hundred percent, bikini-line-glowing naked. Hayden lifted the sheet higher, dreading, *hating* that she must force her glance to the warmth beside her to confirm what she already knew.

Yep. A man. Just as naked. And he was exactly her type. Broad shoulders, nice sprinkling of hair across a muscular chest all leading to a flat stomach and—

Stop right there. How did that gambler's remorse saying go? What happened last night would stay last night.

Only, what *had* happened last night? Hayden rolled to her side, drew her knees up and hugged them to her chest. She massaged tiny circles on her temples, easing away the tension and inviting her memories of last night to take its place.

Still nothing.

What was wrong with her? She didn't feel hungover. Had she been drugged? No, she didn't have that fuzzy, surreal grogginess she'd read about in those PSA pamphlets in college. But clearly something had been done to her; she couldn't remember the night before. Picking up a stranger, getting naked and apparently dancing the horizontal mambo with a guy were usually things she remembered.

She was a commitment girl, in it for the long term when it came to men. Bang and bail wasn't her style.

Hayden glanced over at the man beside her. Her huffing and rustling around in the bed hadn't disturbed him. Maybe whatever had affected her was affecting him, too? Or did he just sleep like the dead on a regular basis?

Don't wait around to find out.

Yes, grabbing her clothes and sneaking out seemed about as obvious as a blinking neon sign. Clearly the only logical response. Okay, no it wasn't. Calmly waking him up and asking him his name and what the hell had happened last night was the only logical response. Hayden just didn't want to do that, and logic had nothing to do with it.

Instead, she flung away the covers, gasping when her own nakedness confronted her again. At least it roused some sense into her.

No, she couldn't sneak out. As tempting as avoidance was, she wouldn't take the coward's path. She needed answers, and the naked man beside her was the only one who could give them to her. Hayden gently tugged the sheet up and secured it around her breasts. She rolled out of bed and gazed down at his face, hoping something would finally click.

If she'd thought his body was droolworthy, his face almost put those washboard abs to shame. Relaxed in sleep and lightly stubbled, the strong curve of his chin, broken by a slight cleft, tempted Hayden to trace her fingers along it. Her gaze lingered on his sensual, full, bottom lip. How many times had she tugged that sexy lower lip of his into her mouth last night? Sucked it?

Tingles shot through her stomach and her nipples hardened against the softness of the sheet. It must have been some night if the man could make her go all tingly when she couldn't remember what he'd achieved with those lips of his.

A shaft of heat shimmied down her back to pool between her legs, but she clamped her knees together. Now was the time for *answers*. Not imagining the hot kisses and slow caresses this man must have delivered last night.

But still, she could steal a moment to gaze down at him. After all, once learning the truth of the night before, she never planned on laying eyes on Mr. I'm Still Sexy After A Night of Wickedness. It was just too weird. One and done wasn't her style.

And yet, last night must have been the toe-curling, forget-all-reason kind of sex, because her skin ached in awareness of him. Desire for more? Obviously her body remembered every caress and kiss and was shouting, *hell yeah—more*. He was the sexy kind of wrong that women lied to themselves to make right. Hayden's heart raced as she neared him and she breathed in his scent. Clean apple, mixed with man and leather and dark, sweet chocolate.

Chocolate? Was she actually comparing him to chocolate? Good Lord, the man *was* addictive. Hayden wanted to breathe him in and taste him all at the same time.

What did I do to this man's body last night?

More like, what hadn't she done? Truth be told, she'd never woken up beside such a delicious man. A thin scar ran across his temple and disappeared into his eyebrow. He possessed a rugged kind of sexiness. Not boyishly handsome, more like *I can make you forget your own name*. He had the kind of dark wavy hair that women loved to drag their fingers through, but which he probably fought to control. She bet his eyes were as dark and beautiful, like a caffe mocha first thing on a cold, rainy morning.

Coffee and chocolate? Clearly she was food deprived. And sleep deprived. *And extra hungry from the workout of last night, perhaps?*

She noticed the lines fanning from his eyes and bracketing his mouth—he smiled a lot. Hayden liked that about him. Which was a relief. She needed to find good things in this man she barely knew but had taken to her bed.

Correction. *A* bed. On top of not recognizing the man, she had no idea where she was. She scanned the room frantically.

She was in a one-room cabin with logs for walls and a wall of windows overlooking a beautiful pond with two ducks playfully swimming and splashing in the water. Completely unfamiliar. What was going on? The ducks wouldn't be giving off any clues, so the only way she'd find out anything was to wake Mr. Hot beside her.

Hayden poked the man in the shoulder. Nothing.

She poked him again, adding a shake and a "Hey!"

His lids slowly opened and locked with hers. Dark brown and just as sexy as she'd suspected. A slow smile spread across his face, and her breath hitched. Then his eyes drifted shut, and that was it. He'd fallen back asleep.

Well, if she wanted him to wake up and stay awake, she'd have to go primal.

TONY'S LIDS OPENED with the force of a kick. Someone was smacking him on the bicep. Hard. In a flash his fingers encircled his attacker's arm, and with a quick yank, he'd subdued and pinned his assailant to the…bed?

He blinked a few times only to see that long brown hair covered the intruder's face, and his fingers were digging into supple, feminine flesh.

"Dammit, woman, I could have hurt you. You can't wake a man up like he's under attack."

He loosened his grip around her wrists, but didn't bother to roll off her body. He was enjoying being exactly where he was. With a soft woman beneath him. Her tight nipples caressing his chest. Her full hips gently cradling the hardness of his cock.

Now this is how to wake up.

She wrested her hands from his light grasp and pushed the hair from her face. "Get. Off. Me."

His eyes met an angry green gaze. A completely unfamiliar green gaze. Holy sh— He backed off her in one fluid motion. Or it was supposed to be smooth. It was more like a jerky, lurching kind of stagger. What the hell had he done last night?

Despite the sluggishness infusing his muscles, Tony didn't feel hungover. No headache. No dry mouth. No dizziness. A rush of sweet relief made his shoulders sag.

He hadn't had a drink in over two years. A vow he planned to keep forever.

Besides, if he had been drinking, he'd be too hungover to now be enjoying the sight of the woman's trim body. An amazing body he'd inadvertently revealed when he'd taken the sheet with him as he'd rolled off her. The roundness of her breasts would fit his hands perfectly. Her rosy nipples hardened before his eyes. And he imagined them hardening further in his mouth. He took in the slight tan lines at her hips and breasts, a treat he was sure few got to see, even though he had absolutely no idea who she was or how she came to be with him.

She gasped at the sudden cold draft of air, her hands flailing around for some protection from his eyes. He gave her a break and turned his back, although with such a stunning woman, he would have already looked his fill last night. Touched his fill. Tasted everywhere.

"Give me the sheet," she ordered. "I don't want you to see me naked."

"What?" he asked with a false appalled tone. "If I gave you the sheet then *you* could see *my* naked ass."

She sighed heavily behind him and he smiled. He couldn't wait to look, touch and taste her—again. His body was ready for round two. Or was it round three? Four?

"Could you just be a gentleman and hand me the sheet."

The strange woman sounded so agitated, Tony instantly felt bad for teasing her. Not that he wasn't rattled by the situation, but he was more relieved that he hadn't fallen off the wagon. "Okay, but you aren't going to like it."

"I'll live," she assured him.

He tossed her the sheet, keeping his eyes averted. He silently counted to ten. Then counted to twenty. He wanted to make sure he gave her plenty of time.

"Uh, you can look now."

When he finally faced her, she sat cross-legged on the largest bed he'd ever seen. The monstrous thing was situated on a platform with filmy white fabric draped across the top of the bed's four posts. Rose petals lay scattered and crushed on the floor and trapped in the bedding.

Discarded towels led to another platform complete with a heart-shaped hot tub. Alarm clenched his gut.

"Are we in the honeymoon suite?" he asked.

"Don't you remember?" she asked.

He slumped on the edge of the mattress. "I don't remember anything. You?"

She shook her head. Then a line formed between her brows. "But you smiled at me this morning. Like you were—" she swallowed "—pleased."

"How's a man supposed to look when he wakes up to a beautiful naked woman plastered against him? Repulsed?"

"I guess not." She hugged the silky sheet to her chest like a life jacket, the ends wrapped around her sweet body. Her full lips were set in a line. Yeah, there'd be no repeat glimpses of the soft curves that had been pressed against him so sweetly only moments before.

Even though she was fully hidden, she glanced everywhere but at his face. He liked that she was shy in the morning. Kind of cute. Then his beautiful stranger lowered her gaze and gasped, quickly averting her eyes.

"I can't believe it."

Yep, she'd spotted his hard cock. "I did warn you that you weren't going to like it if I gave you the sheet."

"Can you please just find your pants?" She peered left then right. "Shouldn't there be a blanket or a comforter around this place? I can't have a conversation with you both looking at me."

Obviously the woman wasn't used to one-night stands. Neither was he, for that matter, but he seemed to be handling it a lot better than she was. "It's not my fault that I woke up next to a gorgeous and naked woman."

"Here." She tossed him a pillow. Very hard. Aimed straight for his crotch.

He caught it at his waist. "Careful."

She lifted a brow. "Really? It's a pillow."

"I wasn't expecting a Spartan-warrior throw."

"Well, Spartans have no place for weakness," she told him, her voice just a notch above a grumble.

He laughed. "Now I know why I picked you up last night. It's a special kind of woman who can quote ancient lore. Okay, now that we're both fully covered, I'm Anthony Garcia, by the way. Documentary filmmaker from California."

"Hayden."

"Hayden, what?"

She shook her head. "No last name until I know more about you."

"Fair enough." He backed up a step, but wariness still flickered in the dark green depths of her eyes. Doubt about him. That he wasn't one of the good guys. Tony flinched.

The cords of his neck tightened. How many times had he been on the receiving end of this exact look? Dozens. Hell, probably hundreds. From teachers. Probably every authority figure he'd come into contact with over the course of his life. Even his own mother. None of them had thought he'd make something of himself. And if Hayden had met him six years ago, she'd be right to flash him that cautious glance.

But he wasn't that Anthony Garcia anymore. And he wanted to prove that to her. "Everyone calls me Tony."

Hayden. He liked knowing her name. And when he got her last name—and he would—he'd show her she had nothing to fear from him.

"And Tony?"

Just the sound of his name on her lips made him need a bigger pillow. Since when had a woman saying "Tony" got him hard? Of course, he'd been working like a dog lately wrapping up the filming of his latest documentary on the cowhands of the Texas plains while researching his next project. There'd been no time for soft curves and sweet smiles.

But obviously he'd decided to end his self-imposed dry spell last night. And it must have been some night. Dammit, why couldn't he remember?

Hayden was the kind of woman a man remembered until he was old and stooped and walking with a cane, and thoughts of her *could still* put a spring in his step.

"Weren't you going to look for your pants?" Her voice cut into his thoughts.

"Right."

Hayden the Mysterious wanted some space, which he understood and would respect because he wasn't a dick. Not anymore. He backed away and once he reached the bathroom, he closed the door behind him with a solid click.

But no clothes were strewn across the tiles or piled in a corner. There were more used towels thrown in a heap on the bathroom floor, though. And the shower was wet. Rose-scented soap rested inside a dish, and he imagined rubbing that soap all over Hayden's body. Her breasts, down her sides and over her ass. He squeezed his eyes shut and breathed through his mouth.

What the hell was the matter with him? He was supposed to be giving her space. Not fantasizing about her beneath the jets of the shower. With a final deep breath he opened his eyes and spotted one lone folded towel on a wooden shelf in the corner of the bathroom. He may not have any answers for Hayden—or himself—yet, but at least he could put her more at ease by covering up. He wrapped the towel around his waist.

Tony wouldn't be surprised if she hadn't already taken off. Bolted away from him as fast as she could given she was wrapped in nothing but a sheet. The idea filled him with panic. Had he already blown his chance to prove to her that he was a good guy? That whatever he had done, he could make it right for her? "Hayden?" he called.

"Yes?"

He blew out a breath of relief.

"No luck in finding our clothes in there?" she asked.

"No, just a couple of empty bottles of apple cider vinegar." He opened the door. "That's weird, right?"

"Maybe not. It's kind of hip right now to rinse your hair with the stuff." She made a sniffing sound. "Come to think of it, I smell it in the air."

"So that's what I've been smelling," he said as he joined her. "Sweet and yet—"

"Almost too strong."

"Exactly."

She'd moved around the cabin as she waited for him

and now stood in front of the large fieldstone fireplace, staring at the dark ash. They must have lit a fire last night, as warmth still emanated from the firebox.

"Looks like we're in a cabin in the woods. I didn't see a car out front. Or our shoes. I'm not sure how we even got here. But there's the key," she told him in a rush, angling her head toward a set of keys on a gold heart-shaped ring on a pink drop-leaf table.

He crossed the room to stand beside her. The softness of her shoulder brushed against his arm, but he would not be distracted.

"Do you see that?" Hayden pointed at something shiny in the cinders.

"Might be one of those metal hooks they put on clothes."

"Yeah, and I think that's the underwire from my bra."

"Why would you burn your bra?"

"Exactly, not my generation."

"Hmm?"

"Never mind. Bad joke." Hayden shook her head. "I really have no idea. Ugh, and that was my favorite bra, too."

"Aren't all bras good?"

She gave him the side eye. "Some you like better than others. Some make your boo— You know, I'm not getting into this with you."

"It's just…my underwear's my underwear."

"If only we could *find* your underwear."

He agreed that while the towel did cover the essential parts, it was still way too intimate.

"But honestly," she glanced at the cooling fireplace

again. "I bet they're in there. Along with the rest of our clothes."

"That could be the metal button on my jeans, and the thing in the back has to be the buckle to my belt."

"And I think that's the fastener on my sandals." Hayden turned away from the fireplace and sat heavily on the flat fieldstones of the raised hearth. "I'm not going to panic about this. I'm not going to panic about this."

"You do realize you're saying that out loud?" he asked.

She lowered her head into her hands, and he felt an overwhelming urge to comfort her. To draw her into his arms and convince her that everything was fine. He stretched out against the flat rock of the fireplace, but the towel parted as he sat and the cold edges of the stones cut into his bare ass. Probably the one and only time in his life he wished he wasn't naked beside a sexy woman.

"Hayden, believe me when I tell you, waking up beside a woman I don't know is new for me, too. I can imagine not remembering scares the hell out of you."

"No, I'm good," she mumbled into her palms.

"Scares the shit out of me." He scrubbed a hand over his stubbled chin. "I haven't handled this right. You *should* be wary of a strange man in your bed. But I promise, I'm a good guy, and I'm going to figure this out."

"We." She sat up and squared her shoulders, and for the first time since waking up she seemed more relaxed.

"What?" he asked.

"*We're* going to figure this out." The barest hint of a

smile touched her face, and his mouth dried. He'd give up his field mic to see that smile aimed at him.

She stood and began to pace in front of him. "Okay, so why would we burn our clothes? There has to be a logical explanation for it."

"Destroying evidence?" he offered.

She stopped midstride and raised a brow at him. "That's your first go-to idea?"

Tony only shrugged.

She continued with her pacing. "Maybe something got on them. Like a toxin or… No, we wouldn't have burned them just so we could breathe in the fumes later when we started the fire. Or maybe burning our clothes is what made us lose our memory in the first place. All the synthetics in the fabrics…"

"Maybe we played Texas Burn 'Em. It's like strip poker, but if you lose on the flop, turn or river, you have to burn an article of clothing."

Hayden's beautiful green eyes first widened then narrowed. "That's not a real game. You're just messing with me now. Besides I don't know how to play Texas Hold 'Em."

"Which is why your clothes are nothing but dust."

"Yours are, too."

"Well, I lost because I'm a gentleman like that."

"Please try not to be charming." More pacing. "I must have had too much to drink last night. I picked you up because I wanted to, and then burned our clothes in some mad fit of passion."

"So now you're the one who picked me up last night?"

She turned toward him, her gaze systematic. "Look

at you—you're the prototype of the guy every woman wants to pick up in a bar. Dark wavy hair, that crooked way you smile that's both endearing and sexy, and c'mon, your body? Seriously, how many ab crunches do you have to perform in a day to get that six-pack?"

"I think I should be offended by that assessment." But why? The woman had just complimented him. But despite having been fully conscious with this amazing woman for less than thirty minutes, he wanted to get to know her better. Explore all her soft curves and remember touching and tasting her this time. And he wanted her to smile at him once as if she wanted to be with him. He didn't want her boxing him in as nothing more than abs, a smile and hair.

Out of nowhere, she made a gasping sound and raced for the bathroom. He surged up and followed her to make sure she was okay. Then he watched as she lowered the sheet and angled her head so she could see her back in the mirror above the sink. Dissatisfied, she shifted, spinning like a dog chasing its tail, alternating between trying to look at her back in the mirror and over her shoulder.

"What are you doing?" he finally asked.

"Checking for the tattoo."

"What? Why?"

"Because that's what people do in these situations, isn't it? Pick up a guy, get a tattoo—it's the crazy night bucket list."

Sexy and funny. He was liking this woman more and more. "I have one thing to say about last night."

"Oh?"

"Can't fault my taste."

Hayden stopped trying to play spot the tattoo and her gaze connected with his. There it was again. The blast of awareness. Her skin exposed above the sheet reddened. A tiny pulse point at the soft spot over her collarbone beat like a wild thing. How did he know her skin was soft? He just knew.

"Now it's weird," she said, her voice low.

"You just told me my smile was sexy."

The briefest of grins touched Hayden's lips, and his heartbeat ratcheted up again because her smile was just what he wanted. "I've decided to roll with it," she said.

Although it violated every instinct hardwired into him, Tony realized they had to find some clothes for her. Get her away from this cabin, the hot tub and the evidence of a wild night of sex. So he could start over.

Start over, and this time get it right and show her he could pull off being a white knight.

OKAY, SO WHAT really was the damage here? She'd just spent the most grueling semester balancing both a full school load and a job. It had taken her six years because she had to work so much, but in two weeks she'd be graduating. So apparently sometime last night she'd decided to cut loose and have a little fun. No harm, no foul.

Now she planned to *roll with it* right out of this cabin and back to reality. She was expecting an offer from one of Dallas's largest engineering firms. But Hastings Engineering had cultivated a reputation of reliability and respectability. And Hayden had seen enough news sto-

ries about people being fired or having to wipe their social media accounts because of one accidental naughty
message or naked selfie going viral.

Alarm swooshed through her. She was naked. She
had a phone. She'd clearly indulged in *something* last
night.

*Don't panic. You wouldn't normally take a naked
selfie, so chances are you didn't last night. But still...*

"We've got to find our phones, Tony. Now. And
somewhere around here has to be our keys. I'm checking by the hot tub."

"I'll take the TV. Too bad this place doesn't have a
coffeemaker."

Coffee sounded like heaven. Something that would
take her mind off what may or may not be stored on the
cloud right now that could torpedo her career before it
even began. No, she had to find that phone. Hayden advanced on the hot tub as if it was a beast blocking her
path to caffeine. The dark red heart-shaped tub lay re-
cessed inside a wooden platform. Burned candles lined
the tub. Good grief, they'd really gone for the romantic cliché. Hell, they hadn't even bothered to drain the
thing.

Too much of a hurry?

Hayden felt her cheeks burning and darted a glance
toward Tony. Wrong move, because right now the towel
was slipping and all she could see was his gorgeous ass.
Maybe that wasn't so bad. Because his ass was muscular
and toned and a treat she wasn't likely to enjoy again.
Maybe she'd had the right idea last night.

If she were to put her new roll-with-it philosophy

to the test, she could drop the bulky sheet at her feet. Cross toward him. Slowly trail her fingertips down the muscular slopes of his back…

Her nipples puckered against the sheet, and the tight hold she had on the restricting barrier slackened. An oh-so-heady, limb-loosening blast of desire rushed through her.

She whirled away from him. Sex with a stranger might have sounded like a good idea at one in the morning. But Hayden had only ever made love to a guy she cared about. Who cared about her. Could she have mind-blowing sex with a stranger? Apparently she had last night. But right now? In the cold light of day when it went against everything she believed at her core?

Tony's not exactly a stranger, the daring side of her brain reminded her. That side of her had been quiet for so long, beaten down by long hours in the library and physically exhausting work in the restaurant that paid her tuition and rent. She couldn't afford a mistake. Not at this point in her life when she was about to make all the dreams for her future now her reality.

Something silver and shiny winked in the sunlight. She pushed one of their discarded red towels aside with her toe to get a better view. It was her favorite hoop earring. She dropped to the floor to pick it up. An inexpensive high school graduation gift from her grandmother, but it was priceless to Hayden. She scooted around the floor trying to find the other earring. She *could not* roll with losing those.

Bingo! There it was. She stretched to reach it.

Tony made a strange choking sound just as she thankfully grabbed the cold metal hoop.

"What?" she asked. Maybe she should be asking *what now?*

"The sheet shifted when you started crawling on the floor, and…I think I found your tattoo."

Hayden's stomach tightened. "Seriously? But I didn't see—"

"It's in a spot, uh, not easily noticed."

The fact that Tony appeared completely uncomfortable was a point in his favor. Hayden took a deep breath. After all, she'd been perfectly resigned to a tattoo five minutes ago. *Yeah, perfectly.*

"Okay, tell me quick, like you're ripping off a bandage. Butterfly, flower or heart?"

"Dragon."

"As in cute, puffy smoke or…?"

"Scales and flame. Medieval. Kind of fierce."

Hayden collapsed against the smooth wood of the hot tub's platform. So much for rolling with it. She began to laugh. "I've always heard tattoos were painful, but I'm not even tender."

A quick two-rap knock on the door startled them both and a voice sounded from the other side. "Good morning, it's Betty from last night."

"Betty?" she mouthed at Tony. His shrug said he had no recollection, either.

"I have your breakfast," Betty said.

"Open the door," he whispered to Hayden as he raced for the bathroom and shut the door. Her stomach had rumbled at the mention of food, so any kind of

I'm-literally-the-girl-with-the-dragon-tattoo meltdown would just have to wait. She tightened the sheet under her arms and made for the door.

A smiling, kind-eyed lady greeted her from the other side of the door. The sun shone brightly behind her and a light breeze ruffled her hair. Birds sang their morning songs in the trees. It was that perfect kind of day that always seemed to spring up when your personal life was completely out of whack.

"I have your breakfast basket right here. Biscuits and gravy, pumpkin spice muffins and a carafe of coffee."

Yes!

She had about a million questions for this woman. But they could wait until after she was dressed. And fed. And without a gorgeous man in her field of vision.

Betty gave her a little smile and leaned in close. "I see the clothes I left for you last night are still here on the porch, so I'll just hand you the basket."

Hayden couldn't hide her cringe. Betty looked as if she could be Hayden's grandma's younger sister, and Hayden felt as if she'd been caught doing something very, very wrong. She shifted her weight from one foot to the other. What must this kind woman think of her?

Of course when she considered this situation rationally, a stranger's opinion shouldn't bother her. *You don't live for others; you live for yourself.*

Blah blah blah. Hayden understood all about the validation trap. That didn't mean she could shake it off easily. It bothered her that Betty assumed Hayden had been apparently way too intent on the man in her bed last night to even employ the ten seconds it would take to grab a bag of donated clothes.

Nothing like that would ever bug the other young women in her engineering classes. But then, most of them hadn't been raised by grandparents who seemed old-fashioned even to people of their own generation. In a word, she was mortified.

Betty's voice lowered. "Sorry again about not being able to find a bra in your size, but there's an extra cami in the pile so you can layer." Then she flashed Hayden a comforting smile and the embarrassment and awkwardness churning inside her vanished.

Hayden loved Betty in that moment. The woman would be in her will. If she ever wrote a book, it would be dedicated to her. But coffee or clothes, which was more important?

"Thanks," she gushed to their host as she took the basket.

Betty handed her the small mesh grocery bag with the clothes that had been left for them the night before. "Bill has your car down by our cabin. He's gotten most of the smell out, but, you know, humans never win when they face a skunk."

"Huh? Oh, yes, so true."

"But it was so sweet of you to save the dog, although it wouldn't have been the first time he's lost a battle with a skunk, too." Betty turned to leave. "Oh, and checkout was at noon. But since you guys didn't get here until after ten last night, and we don't have any other bookings, feel free to stay until two."

Hayden closed the heavy oak door and leaned her

head against the smooth wooden surface. Then she realized she'd missed the opportunity to find out more from the woman. "I was going to ask so many questions," she mumbled.

"You still can," Tony said as he emerged from the bathroom, still looking as gorgeous as when she'd woken up in his arms. Still same towel low on his hips. Surely that bag contained some sanity-saving pair of pants he could wear.

Still, she couldn't handle any more conversations with Mr. Should Be a Model for *Pec and Ab Magazine*. She thrust the sack of clothes into his hands.

"You can get dressed first," she offered, sounding way too cheerful and helpful.

A small smile played about those beautiful lips of his. Did he suspect she wanted, no *needed* him to be covered?

The attraction she had to this man was puzzling. Hayden didn't believe in love at first sight. Not even love after six months. But she did believe in possibilities. And pleasure. And she knew the man leaning against the wall could give her both.

"Hayden?" Something heated and primal flickered in his dark gaze. Her heartbeat slowed. He pushed off the wall with his shoulder and crossed toward her.

Beat.

A shaft of sunlight blazed across his magnificent body, and she noticed the word *fearless* tattooed across his bicep.

Beat.

He stopped a foot away, towering over her. Big. Strong.

Beeaaatttt.

Her breath hitched and his eyes narrowed at her gasp.

"Do I frighten you, Hayden? Say the word and I'm out of here."

She was all kinds of afraid of how he made her feel. But no, that wasn't what he'd asked. She shook her head.

"Then give me your hand."

Her hand balled up into a fist for a moment, then she lifted her arm. He clasped her fingers in his grip, strong and sure. His head lowered a fraction, as if he was going to kiss her. Hayden's lips parted in anticipation, and the slow cadence of her heart flipped, now ratcheting up in speed. She spotted want and need in his gaze—and regret. He stopped.

Disappointment razored through her. He was going to give her space.

"Coffee," she told him. "Everything's better after coffee." Tony didn't drop her hand, and instead walked beside her toward the table where she'd stashed the breakfast from Betty. "Oh, I almost forgot. Apparently we lost a fight with a skunk last night."

"That explains the burned clothes and bottles of apple cider vinegar." Tony released her hand to rummage through the bag of clothes.

"I'll unload our breakfast while you change. In the bathroom." It was an act of self-preservation. She couldn't handle Tony dressing in front of her after that near kiss.

"Yes, explains the clothes…but not the hot tub," he told her as he shut the door, his voice low and setting off a chain reaction of awareness in every part of her body.

Nope, it did not explain the hot tub. Nor that path of towels to the platform bed. Hayden felt her face heat for about the hundredth time. Her skin was probably growing all blotchy. She never handled embarrassment well.

Hayden opened the wicker basket Betty had delivered and pulled out a coffee carafe and mugs. She quickly poured two cups, and then took a long draw from the mug, so glad the brew wasn't piping hot because she would have gulped it down, burned tongue or not.

She was reaching for the carafe to top off her cup when Tony emerged from the bathroom dressed in jean shorts and a T-shirt announcing I Do A Body Good.

"Oh, if only I could remember," she teased, surprised she'd so quickly slid into a playful mood. Coffee did a body good, too.

"Don't laugh. Your shirt is worse," he said, tossing her a bright pink T-shirt with Too Hot To Handle across the chest.

"Betty and her husband must have an interesting sense of humor," she said as she raced for the bathroom to change.

Fifteen minutes later, Hayden no longer had to walk with a bedsheet trailing behind her like a train. She dumped the sheet on the straightened bedding. Betty's bag had also provided her a change of underwear, the promised cami and a pair of khaki shorts. After a quick finger comb to her hair, she joined Tony at the table. The enticing scent of pumpkin spice muffin was too much and she reached into the basket and plopped a piece into her mouth. Delicious.

They sat in silence for a moment. They needed to have a conversation, but what was the protocol here? She'd missed the How to Talk to the Stranger You Just Slept With etiquette lesson. Of course avoidance was the preferred course of action in any social situation. A lesson taken straight from her grandma. Hayden bit back a smile as she remembered the woman's advice. *Hayden, dear, don't force it. Things have a way of working themselves out, you'll see.*

Now people would call that "escape coping," but sometimes Grandma was right and things did work themselves out.

In other words, just roll with it. Yes, that's exactly what she'd do.

But first, one piece of information was best not avoided. For both their sakes. "You don't have to worry about pregnancy or anything. I'm covered there."

Alarm flashed through his brown eyes. "Hell, I hadn't even thought about that yet."

"Too busy trying to figure out how to ditch me?" she joked.

"No. Too busy trying to figure out what kind of idiot forgets making love to the most beautiful woman he's ever been with."

She let out a small laugh, but Hayden was torn. Torn because she didn't know how to feel. All her emotions warred with each other as if they were battling for the last brownie in the pan. She was mortified that she couldn't remember last night. Thrilled that she'd connected with Mr. Amazing and Hot. She was a contradictory mess of embarrassment, satisfaction and chagrin. And Tony thought *he* was the idiot. "I guess I'm strangely flattered."

Tony leaned toward her, his brown eyes intent. "We have two options. Go our separate ways and forget this ever happened. Or find out why we hooked up and why neither of us can remember it."

"*How* we hooked up. I know *why*."

A slow smile curved his gorgeous lips. Tony had mentioned he was a filmmaker. Cue the rainbow. And the birds chirping. Hell, bring in a unicorn because at this moment all the embarrassment and mortification vanished. "I don't even know where we are," she said, breathless.

"The back of that take-out menu says Broken Bow, Oklahoma," he told her, nodding to a couple of menus stuck to a bulletin board with tacks near the kitchen sink. Yeah, the couples who stayed in this lover's cabin probably didn't plan to venture out during their whole stay. Drop the supplies at the door and go was more likely their approach once they spotted that heart-shaped tub and platform bed.

"Uh, the last place I remember is Texas," she said.

"Dallas?" he asked and she nodded. "There's a start. We must have met in Dallas. Of course, I can't even figure out how to get back there because I still can't find my phone."

"Same. Do you have a map in your car?"

Tony flashed her an embarrassed glance, so Hayden knew the answer was no. Her grandparents had embraced technology as much as the next person, but when it came to navigation, Grandma Taylor insisted on paper. Every year, she gifted Hayden with a new and updated atlas in case technology failed. But Betty had only mentioned one car, and chances were that it was his.

"Maybe Betty can loan us a map," he offered. "Or we can stop at a gas station on the way out of town. You in?"

Was she? Hayden could only do damage control if she knew exactly what she'd done last night. And that meant she had to stick with Tony. "Yes—we have a plan," she said, hopeful for the first time that day.

Five minutes later they stepped out together on the wooden planked porch. Two rocking chairs swayed in the breeze. In the distance, the trees loomed tall and lush, so different from the flat terrain of Texas where she'd grown up. Two hawks flew a lazy pattern above her head and the sound of locusts filled the air.

She pointed out two squirrels chasing each other around the trunk of a tree. "You know what's strange? I've lived in Texas all my life, and have never been to Oklahoma. You'd think at least once I would have crossed the border."

"I've never been to Oklahoma, either. Something we have in common."

"Tony, I bet's that's how we ended up here," she told him, gripping his arm. The muscles beneath her fingertips bulged. "I can't believe how excited I am to realize that."

"It sucks not feeling in control. Not knowing what you've done."

Something dark and regretful lurked in his tone—as

if he'd weathered a similar situation in his past. She gave his arm a squeeze before dropping her hand down to her side. Until this moment, Tony had been teasing or reassuring. But since waking up, she'd only been concerned about herself. Hayden hadn't given a second thought to how he must be feeling. Instead, she'd pegged him as *that dude*—the kind of man who congratulated himself on getting lucky. But there was more to him than that.

"I've been kind of a bitch to you, haven't I?" she asked as they approached a larger cabin marked Office.

He gave her a wink. "It's okay—I can handle a few knocks."

Hayden laughed as the front door opened and Betty walked out to greet them. "Hey, you two lovebirds. That's just the way you were last night. Covered in stink but still laughing. Although you smell so much better this morning, but it's nice to see the smiles are still there."

"Thanks for helping us out. We didn't seem, uh, strange to you last night?"

Betty just laughed. "Honey, you were covered in skunk, of course you seemed strange. But no odder than any other high-on-love couple."

High on...what?

"We didn't leave our phones with you?" Tony asked.

"No, just the car. Mike's bringing it around now. Maybe you left your phones in the car. By the way, I used my homemade air freshener in it last night and again this morning. Lilac and pine. Between that and the breeze, I think you're good."

Car tires crunched on the gravel and they all turned

to watch a bright red car with black polka dots painted on it—it was a ladybug on wheels. "That's your car?" she whispered.

"I was hoping that was yours," he groaned.

Oh, crap.

She'd had about a million questions to ask Betty and Mike and every single one of them vanished the moment a ladybug car neither of them owned rolled toward them. Mike slid out of the car and handed Tony the keys. Ugh, as if the keys belonged in Tony's hand.

"That's a tight squeeze, Tony. Not sure how you're comfortable wedged behind the steering wheel. But anything for the ladies, huh?" Mike asked as he draped an arm around Betty's shoulders and kissed her temple.

"Oh, well…" Tony mumbled.

Get out of here. Now. Before Mike and Betty began to ask questions that would lead to 9-1-1, handcuffs and a single phone call. Hayden didn't know which was worse. The prospect of that jailhouse phone call or that she really had no one to phone. She might as well dial the HR person at Hastings Engineering because she definitely wouldn't be working there after she was arrested.

She swiped the keys from Tony's hands. "Actually, I do most of the driving. He's the navigator."

The other couple laughed.

"Speaking of navigating, you wouldn't happen to have an extra map?" Tony asked.

Mike nodded. "Follow me. I think I might have one in the garage."

Betty handed Hayden a small bag as they watched

the two men walk away. "Some homemade cookies for the road."

"Thanks," she told her, distracted by Tony's muscular legs and firm—

"Uh-huh." The other woman smiled.

Had she just been caught staring at a man's ass? By someone who could be her grandma?

"Glad it goes both ways between you two. That boy is enchanted by you. He's a keeper."

Hayden didn't know which was more startling. A six-foot plus man being referred to as a boy or that he'd appeared *enchanted* by her. What a sweet word. How would it feel to have a man like Tony enchanted by her? Very agreeable as long as they were using words Jane Austen would write.

"Yeah, he's something."

Hayden slid into the driver's seat as Mike and Tony rounded the corner, map in hand. At least that was one problem they'd been able to solve.

Tony joined her in the car with a strained smile. Oh yeah, they were driving off in a car that neither of them owned.

"Did we steal this car last night?" she asked through clenched teeth that hopefully looked like a smile to the waving Mike and Betty.

"I'm going with we just borrowed it from a new acquaintance, since no one I know drives a ladybug car." He glanced up from the map as she shifted the car into Drive and headed down the gravel path. "I'm assuming none of your friends do, either?"

She shook her head.

"According to the map, this is a private road that winds through the trees for about a mile. Pull over when you no longer see Betty and Mike's fence line."

Hayden drove another quarter of a mile until the friendly white fence turned to barbed wire. "Maybe we stashed our phones in the glove box," she suggested as she pulled off the main road and put the car in Park.

Tony twisted the knob and as the glove box sprang open, dozens of green bills plopped onto his lap. "Holy shit." Several more stacks of neatly piled cash remained in the glove box. "There has to be at least two thousand dollars in here."

"I'm hoping that's yours," she said, afraid to hear the answer with the way their morning began. Her bank account currently sat at a nice, minimum-deposit requirement of fifty bucks.

He shook his head. "Nope. Your guess as to where this came from is as good as mine."

Her throat began to tighten. "We've got to ditch the car. Wipe it down. Remove all trace evidence we were even here," she told him, desperately trying to recall helpful hints from every crime movie she'd watched in the past decade. "Maybe we can give the rest of the cash to Mike and Betty so they forget they even saw us."

Tony reached for her hands and drew them into his. "Hayden, would you normally steal a car?"

She exhaled in a deflated hiss. "Well, no."

There was that reassuring smile of his again. "Something weird happened to us last night, but we wouldn't do one-eighties on our personalities."

She relaxed against the seat cushion. That was the first really good news she'd had since the coffee.

"Our phones aren't in the glove box. Maybe we put them in the trunk to keep them safe," he said, as he reached for the door handle.

"If we weren't worried about stashing the money in the car, I doubt we would have been worried about the phones."

"True, but I'll check anyway."

She popped the trunk so he could search. A minute later he crouched outside her window. "Nope, nothing."

The sun glinted off his dark hair. She really wanted to touch it. Run her fingers through it. It would help to take her mind off their situation. Of course it also helped that he was such an easy distraction. What was it he'd said about himself? Couldn't fault his taste? Yeah. Same here, buddy.

"Tony, I might steal a car if the circumstances really warranted it." Where had that sobering thought come from? Wherever it had originated, she wanted to shut that part of her brain down before her mind added any other irritating revelations.

"Only after you left a note and promised to return it with a full tank," he told her with a wink.

She pulled a piece of fluff off her shorts. "Well, that goes without saying."

"Hayden."

His voice gently urged her to look up. She raised her gaze to his and sucked in a breath. Something heated and elusive stirred inside her.

The humor faded from his eyes and he stiffened. "You feel it, too."

She could only nod, and twisted in her seat so she could stare down the road and not at him. Her heart raced and her mouth was dry; she was having a serious case of want.

Hayden's grandma was fond of sayings about closed doors leading to open windows—this morning had felt very much as if she'd run into a closed door, but that smile of his was like a fresh breeze through an open window.

"Hayden, I don't want to get back to the city and forget all about this…this thing between us. I don't know what it is, but I know it doesn't happen. At least not to me."

"Me, either," Hayden admitted. She glanced his way, memorized every part of his strong profile because she didn't want to forget this beautiful man. But then she didn't really have to. She wasn't playing the avoidance game this time. Last night, call it instinct or lack of inhibitions, but *something* had drawn her to this man. And so far that hadn't been misplaced; he'd proven to be concerned for her and had given her space when she'd needed it.

Oh, Hayden could tell herself she'd stick with Mr. Abs because it was an adventure or that she wanted to make sure there weren't any, er, indiscreet pictures that could derail her career, but if she were being truthful, intuition also told her she didn't have to be guarded around this man.

She got out of the car to stand beside him. "Let's find out what happened to us," she said.

He flashed her that amazing smile of his and her skin grew warm. Memories of waking up in his strong arms and feeling the heat of his naked body against hers flooded her senses. Made her nipples tingle. But she had no memory of kissing him, breathing him in and tasting him. She wanted to change that. Right. Now.

"We could always do the old trick of making out to jog our memory," he suggested, his voice playful.

She lifted a brow. "That's an old tactic, is it?"

He nodded. "Tried and true, dates back way before the Jazz Age—"

Hayden cut off his words with her lips. He stood there rigid, his mouth unmoving. Then his arm encircled her waist, drawing her flush against his body. She pressed against him, and he groaned. His lips parted and she slipped her tongue inside his mouth, tasting coffee and pumpkin and something delicious that could just be Tony.

"You taste good," she whispered against his lips.

"So do you. Amazing. Um…not that I'm complaining, but *that* came out of nowhere."

"Not that you'd believe me, but I don't usually indulge in my impulsive side. But any guy who uses the Jazz Age as an excuse to make out is a man I'd try to jog my memory with."

"Actually I know all kinds of history," he told her with a wink.

"All except ours. Speaking of…? Did you remember anything? I got nothing."

He made a faux flinching movement that was too charming. "You got nothing? Surely I was better than that."

She patted his arm. "Oh, you were a lot better—okay no. I'm not falling for that ruse. I'm keeping my opinions of your kiss to myself."

"How will I know if I'm doing it right?" he asked, all innocence. Yeah, like this man held any doubts about his technique.

Hot. Sensual. Carnal. And those were just the first three words that popped into her head to describe the kiss. "I'll tell you what, if I come back for more, then you'll know if you're doing it right."

"Fair enough." He eyed the front seat. "As uncomfortable as this car is, I think I should drive."

"Why?" she asked.

His eyes softened, and a rueful smile touched his lips. "Because if we're caught I can make them believe you had no idea I'd stolen the car. Only one of us gets arrested."

It was strangely chivalrous. Hayden reached up, sank her fingers into the hair at the nape of his neck so she could draw him nearer. The reality of his kiss was way better than the fantasy.

"Besides," he said, his gaze dropping from hers to study something far off in the distance. "I've been in jail before."

2

JAIL. BEFORE?

Hayden's hands fell.

"Yeah. That usually does it," he told her, his voice tired. Tony turned away from her and just like that, the figurative window slammed shut, too.

She squinted against the sunshine as she tried to read his body language. Back straight and hands fisted at his sides. Didn't need that one lone psychology class to diagnose him as tense and agitated.

Had she been too quick to trust him? Was he really an ax murderer or the mastermind of a Ponzi scheme? What she needed was answers. And maybe an escape route.

Okay, before she got all weird about this, people were arrested all the time for bizarre stuff. Not returning a library book for twenty years. Changing the clothes on a mannequin in full view of the public. She'd even heard a crazy story about how a police officer had dragged a lady—with her toddler strapped to the car seat—right to the clinker, all for a few days' expired driver's license.

Did people still use words like *clinker*?

Focus.

People also got arrested for grand theft auto, burglary or kidnapping. Check. Check. And check?

She could reach for his hand and talk this out with him, or reach for the keys and zoom down the road away from him. Both made sense. But if Tony had planned to hurt her, he must be pretty inept because he'd really missed his chance. In fact, when he'd had the opportunity, he'd kept his distance, had in fact taken near-Herculean efforts to avoid touching her and done everything a man could do to put her at ease in what must have been an incredibly awkward situation for him, too.

He turned as she approached him, her footsteps crunching the leaves and twigs scattered along the side of the road. He towered above her, and when his brown eyes met hers, they gave no hint of his thoughts.

"I'm so used to the people around me being aware of my past, that I forget how people can judge."

Okay, that was defensive—and an overreaction. "Listen, I've known you, what? Half an hour fully clothed? No one makes good decisions naked. Besides, you don't get to casually throw out that you were in prison, and then get all sensitive when I'm nervous about it. Understandably nervous."

He sucked in a deep breath and his brow furrowed. This must be deep-in-thought Tony. Considering she'd only known him half an hour—fully clothed—she'd already seen him, chivalrous, considerate, playful and very, very naughty.

Or was that naked. Definitely naked.

Focus.

"You're right," he said.

"What's your angle here?"

Tony shook his head, but a small smile toyed with that übersexy lower lip of his. "You are the suspicious one. No angle, just truth."

Then he shrugged.

A shrug? As if what he'd said was no big deal? Hayden had never thought of herself as the suspicious type, but what kind of man tells a woman she's right? Things weren't adding up.

"So you're saying you were wrong a moment ago?" she asked, just to make sure she'd heard him correctly.

Tony nodded, then ran his palms down the denim material of his borrowed shorts. "Hayden, this doesn't have to be so hard. Take the car. Take the cash. I can walk into town. Just leave me enough money to make a call at a pay phone somewhere."

"Do they still even have pay phones?"

"I'll figure something out. Don't worry about me. I don't think we stole the money or the car, but make your first stop in town at the police station if you're worried."

His eyes were clear, and that gorgeous smile of his was honest. She spotted nothing but openness, and her lips pursed together. "You're trying to convince me you're a good guy, aren't you?" she asked after a long moment.

He rubbed at the stubble on his chin. "After a whole lot of work, I am a good guy."

"And prison?"

"Technically it was jail. And that's a story best left to tell you on the long road trip to Dallas." Playful, sexy Tony was back.

"So what you're saying is that I'll learn all your secrets if I don't strand you on the side of the road."

He leaned toward her, bringing with him the scent of sunshine and pure masculine temptation. "Maybe not *all* my secrets." His voice was a teasing rasp that made her want to surrender to that temptation. A challenge urging her on—*yeah, go ahead and try to learn all my secrets.*

"I have conditions," she warned.

"Lay 'em on me."

"We don't spend the money except on essentials. Like gas. Not until we know the cash is ours free and clear." Truthfully, she didn't believe they'd stolen the money, either. It just wasn't in her nature, and it would risk way too much to ever make taking a couple of thousand dollars worth it. The real Hayden, the one who'd still managed to hook up with a protective sexy man despite a night of craziness would never have pocketed this cash. But borrowing wasn't completely out of the realm of possibilities, and loans meant repayment. Debt didn't even begin to describe the kind of bills awaiting her after graduation and gainful employment. No sense in adding to her balance by spending needlessly on the return trip to Dallas.

"Agreed. The money stays safe."

"Don't lie to me. Ever."

"Been lied to before?" he asked.

Her sigh was heavy. "Lots of times."

"So you've been lied to and apparently have a problem with always being right. You need to date better men, Hay."

Don't I know it. "And don't call me Hay."

He lifted a brow. "That's the third condition?"

"People think it's really funny to text me that. *Hey, Hay.*"

"It could be worse."

Hayden shook her head. "It's become a favorite nickname for my friends. It's obnoxious."

He kissed the end of her nose, and she shivered. "Okay, no *hey, Hay.*"

The third condition had originally been that he keep his hands to himself. Despite whatever had happened the night before, she *was* a responsible adult. An engineer. Almost. People depended on her to design roads and bridges and lines that delivered water and power and heat to their homes reliably. Or would.

She took comfort in being reliable and dependable. It was the way her grandparents raised her to be. Informing a man she barely knew that sex was off the table for the foreseeable future was most definitely the responsible thing to do.

There are other kinds of reliable, her subconscious teased. Like a man who could be relied upon for a good time. If Tony could give her shivers with just an almost-innocent kiss on the nose, imagine what he could do with his hands? His lips? His whole body? *Depend-*

able orgasms, that's what. "Yeah, no *hey, Hay*. That's my third condition."

"I drive, you navigate?" he asked with a nod.

"It's sweet of you to offer, but it's really okay. Especially since the car is so uncomfortable." Hopefully he wasn't one of those men who didn't want the woman to drive.

"I also figured you wouldn't want to drive the whole distance, and since you know the Dallas area better than I do, you could take that leg of the trip."

"Okay, sounds like a plan, Mr. uh—what's your last name?" Yeah, very responsible. She'd just been considering orgasms with a man whose last name was a blank.

"Garcia. I told you that earlier, remember?" He opened the passenger door for her and she slumped down hard against the seat.

Garcia. Documentary filmmaker. She'd refused to share her last name. "Oh, yeah, I do now." She rubbed at her temples as if that would snap the events of the past twenty-four hours back into place. "My short-term memory is fuzzy."

"Same with me," Tony informed her as he slid behind the wheel. He rolled the seat almost all the way back to accommodate his legs and turned the ignition to fire up the car. "What did you eat for breakfast?"

"Pumpkin spice muffins and biscuits with a load of gravy," she told him, no temple rubbing needed. "No problem remembering that. I'm guessing whatever was responsible for taking our memories of last night was mostly out of our systems by the time we ate." Or food played way too much of a role in her life to be forgotten. Probably both.

Tony's fingers tapped against the steering wheel as he drove. "Okay, so we have memory loss. What about that fire-breathing tattoo? Still no discomfort?"

Just the kind one got from knowing she had a dragon permanently drawn on her butt. And knowing that Tony had seen it, scales and all. But no, it wasn't painful. She wiggled around in her seat just to be sure. "Still nothing."

"Memory loss and pain relief. Could be anything."

They broke out of the trees and Tony turned on his blinker to merge onto the state highway. Billboards advertising diners and roadside motels greeted them along a lonely stretch of road.

This rural part of Oklahoma didn't look that much different from Texas—blue skies and flat plains dotted with cows and horses stretched to the horizon.

Silence settled between them, edgy and filled with so many unanswered questions. They'd been go-go-go since they'd woken up this morning, and now there was time to think. Time to feel. Although her memory of last night was gone, and her recall of this morning sketchy, her body sure did remember sensation. Touch. Taste. She craved more. More of Tony. Her nipples pebbled and Hayden crossed her arms against her chest.

"How about some tunes?" she suggested, her mouth dry. Maybe once they found a town, they could stop at a convenience store and grab a couple bottles of water and she could cool down.

Tony played around on the radio, trying to find a sta-

tion, but he only got static and a lone swap-meet pro-
gram. He quickly switched it off when it became clear
all the offerings would be farm related.

"I guess the state car license-plate game is out," she
offered with a small laugh, trying to make light of the
situation.

He shook his head, and his eyes crinkled with a
smile. "The only car for the past ten miles was going
the other way."

"When I was little, my grandma and I would play
two truths and a lie."

"Now that doesn't seem fair."

"Oh?"

"I promised I'd never lie, and I always keep my
promises, Hayden."

A delicious tingle of sensation trembled down her
spine and settled in the small of her back. Snippets of
their conversation from this morning, hazy though they
might be, filtered into her mind.

I promise, I'm a good guy.

*What kind of idiot forgets making love to the most
beautiful woman he's ever been with?*

*I don't want to get back to the city and forget all
about this.*

Even working a double at the diner couldn't have pre-
vented her from ignoring the heady stuff he was tossing her way. Ripples of want tumbled through her body.
Yeah, she definitely wanted a repeat of last night—only
this time she was determined to remember it. But first
she wanted to find out more about the man she was
going to romp on later.

"So…um…jail."

He chuckled, low and rumbly, which predictably bombarded her with a new layer of want. Why was she so into this guy? Great looking, sure. Smart and funny, true. But she'd dated other men bearing the lethal three before. Sometimes all even in the same guy.

Pheromones?

The mystery?

She almost snapped her fingers. The mystery of him— that had to be it. How they'd hooked up coupled with his shadowy past, how could she resist?

"That's not a story I tell to people I barely know."

She rolled her eyes. "Oh, come on. You've seen me naked. You know me well enough."

Tony glanced her way, his dark eyes meeting hers, and then dropping to her lips. Her breasts. She sucked in a breath. He fixed his gaze on the highway again, his knuckles whitening as he gripped the steering wheel. Hard.

Good. She didn't want to be the only one battling against the collapse of common sense due to hot sexual vibes.

"It's probably the same story with hundreds of kids. I didn't fit in. No one gave a shit at home. I was angry about everything for no reason and for a thousand reasons all at the same time. I'd been labeled a trouble-maker back in high school."

His sigh was heavy, self-deprecating and yet indicating a distance from his old self in a way. Great. Hot, sexy *and* contradictory.

"One day I ditched school and took my mother's car."

"What did you do?" Although it probably made her sound like the biggest bore out of Boresville, she'd have no idea what to do if she stole a car. Try to hide it for later? Rob something else?

"Just drove around with the music loud. I thought I was pretty damn cool, bucking the system and messing with my mom, until I sideswiped a car."

"Oh, no."

"Well, I was barely fifteen so it was bound to happen. I was arrested, but the cops only locked me in an interrogation room and played a bad-cop-badder-cop scenario, probably to try to scare me straight. But I was hell-bent on a path of destruction. They ran the plates and called my mom. I could hear her voice as she talked to the police officer. She asked if they had a jail cell. 'Put him in it,' she'd told them."

"Tough love."

"Just tough." He rubbed his fingers along the stubble on his chin. A tell? That was the second time he'd made that gesture.

"There are days when I actually feel sorry for my mom. Had to have been tough, pregnant at sixteen and dropping out of school. Her parents—I won't even call them my grandparents—kicked her out of the house when she refused to put me up for adoption. My bio dad was off impregnating some other girl by the time I was born. My mom always had great intentions and even bigger illusions. I'm sure she was imagining I'd be that one bright spot in her life to give her unconditional love."

Hayden had always believed that to be the parents'

job. Her mom and dad had died young, but she'd always known they'd loved her. Same with Gran and Grandpa, who'd delayed their early retirement plans to raise her.

"Instead she got a carbon copy of herself. Moody, defiant and forever rebellious. I actually think those cops felt bad as they locked me up."

"How long did you stay in there?"

"Long enough to get a black eye from another inmate and to realize I wasn't as tough as I thought I was, but that lesson didn't stick. A few hours later, someone from Children's Services came to take me to juvie."

She tried to imagine Tony as a scared teenager whose mother hadn't loved him, and Hayden's heart and emotions and everything girlie inside her began to soften and melt.

Don't. Don't do it. You are not his rescuer who is going to show him true love and give him hope. He is not going to be a better man all because of the woman who sees past the tough, hard facade he's erected to barricade his heart from the cold, unfeeling world.

That dreamy scenario didn't even work in movies anymore. She didn't believe in others saving you. You saved yourself. Besides, he seemed to be doing just fine.

"How long were you in juvie?"

"A week and a half. I got probation and a promise that my record would be expunged if I kept my nose clean. Ha—that didn't last long. My mother was ordered to take parenting classes that she attended drunk. So yeah, storybook family of the year we were not."

"What was your big turnaround then, because clearly you're…"

His eyes crinkled at the corners again. "What?"

"Um."

"Hot? Funny? Sexy?"

"Actually, I was going to say doing pretty okay."

"The word every man wants to hear from the woman who woke up naked beside him. *Okay.*"

Hayden gave him a playful shrug. "Maybe if I'd had something to remember from last night…"

"Whoa. You're going to play it like that."

Actually, she'd had no idea how she was going to play it until that near dare rushed out of her mouth.

"Almost sounds like the lady is issuing a challenge."

Dependable orgasms.

The subconscious thought popped up and threatened to derail her common sense. But what was the downside here? Tony was hot, clearly understood boundaries and as he lived in California, he'd be gone soon. So maybe he was the perfect candidate for a little pregraduation celebratory fling.

"Maybe it is a challenge."

Tony's right hand dropped from the steering wheel and he reached for her hand. His fingers twined through hers, warm and strong. His knuckles grazed her thigh and little goose bumps tingled to life.

"Challenge accepted."

3

"So HOW'D YOU go from juvie to documentary film-maker?" she asked, her fingers still entwined with his. Project Getting To Know The Man You Plan To Romp On Later was officially in effect.

"You'd think the world would be easy for a mouthy guy with a piss-poor attitude, a distrust of anyone in authority and a confrontational approach at school. That is, when I attended school."

Hayden laughed, which she was supposed to do. Fact to file—Anthony Garcia liked to cover up hard memories and pain with humor.

"By the time I was a sophomore, I was ditching school more than I ever went. One of Mom's boyfriends thought it was funny to change the locks and so I stopped going home altogether."

She gave his hand a light squeeze, and he squeezed hers right back.

Warmth. Understanding. Connection.

"Probation doesn't last when you're found squatting

in rentals, blowing off school and getting high. They dragged me in before the same judge from before and she gave me a choice. Jail or the CW Transitional Center. I was almost stupid enough to say jail, because self-destruction was a way of life for me by then. Another one of the few things I shared with my mom. But the center was my last shot, and something inside me made me keep my idiot mouth shut. I remember the first day there, I— Damn! Would you look at that."

Hayden straightened in her seat and glanced left and right but only saw the outlying indicators of a small town. Gas station, a roadside strip hotel and a car dealership. "What?" she asked.

"There's my car." He pointed to a sleek navy roadster, older but obviously well loved, parked in front of the dealership. Brightly colored helium balloons were tied to the side mirrors and a large placard announcing For Sale was stretched across the dashboard. "Or that *was* my car."

Tony flipped on the blinker and pulled the Ladybug into the row of spaces outside the floor-to-roof glass windows advertising no credit checks, 0 percent down and low cost financing.

A man sporting the smooth fabric of a very expensive dress shirt and a muted silk tie shoved open the door and scurried toward them.

Hayden stifled a groan. She'd rather give up chocolate for a month than step on a car lot. Who loved feeling stressed, pressured and patronized? She hated buying anything that didn't have a set price anyway, and salesmen seemed especially adept at locating and zeroing in on her weaknesses, ensuring she got the worst possible deal available every time.

"We need some kind of a plan before we get out," Tony said.

"When he comes up to us, no matter what he says… just act natural. Like it's absolutely normal for us to be here today."

His lips twisted and he raised a brow. "You're really good at this whole subterfuge business."

"It's all I got," she told him with a shrug.

"Works for me. Unless…" His voice lowered, and he looked behind his shoulder quickly.

"Unless what?"

"How natural should we react when the police pull up beside us because we took this car for a test drive last night and never came back? Or maybe we just walked around the dealership and snatched the keys from someone's desk and ran. Damn, I shouldn't have parked so far away from the exit."

Her chest constricted in alarm. "Tony, why in the world did you pull in here? Forget your old car. Put Ladybug in Reverse and gun it."

Then she spotted the playful twinkle in his eyes. "Okay, cut it out," she demanded with a wag of her finger. "I know you're messing with me. Are you sure it's documentaries you make? With that imagination maybe you should be writing films."

"Well, those two scenarios did cross my mind. There was a time in my life when…" His words trailed off.

"Oh, stop it." She had another fact to add to the file marked Project Getting To Know The Man You Plan

To Romp On Later—Tony liked to tease. She'd squirrel that away for later and simply enjoy the moment of appreciating his playful smile. Yeah, before they were arrested, because it would all be downhill from there.

He engulfed both her hands in his, his palms warm and comforting. "I'm positive you wouldn't steal a car, Hayden. And just to reassure you, my lawless days went the way of my baggy cargo shorts and soul patch. I'm a good guy now."

That was the second time he'd assured her he was one of the good ones. Clearly, her knowing that was important to him. Although she hoped he wasn't too good.

She reached for the door handle. "I guess now's the time to see our fate."

The smile slowly faded from his face and the teasing glint vanished from those deep, dark eyes of his as he looked at her. "I see my fate."

Her heart pounded in her chest and her chin would have dropped if he hadn't suddenly winked and opened his door.

"Ah, Tony. So glad you've come by again. Is Hayden with you?" asked the approaching salesman, with both hands in the air in welcome. Ah, yes, already in pretend best-friend mode. At least he wasn't secretly pocket dialing the police for help.

Hayden's shoulders slumped and her breath came out in one long, relieved hiss. No way would they be greeted so enthusiastically if they'd done anything illegal last night. Tony glanced her way and gave her a wink as if to say, *told you it'd all work out.*

"And the car looks…interesting," the salesman managed to say.

Poor Ladybug. Even a man trained to lie for a living couldn't give the girl a real compliment. Hayden climbed out of the car and joined the two men inspecting the black dots on the shiny red hood.

Their salesman sported a lanyard proclaiming his name was Jeff and he'd been salesman of the year three quarters ago. Jeff scratched at his head. "I wasn't sure how well the touch-up paint would work making the spots, but it came out pretty much how I imagined." Still not a compliment. "Did you use all six bottles?"

Tony and Hayden looked at each other. "Hayden, I don't remember, did we?"

Great, thanks, funny guy. That was his idea of playing it normal?

She nodded her head with a smile. "We sure did. Isn't it pretty?"

"It's something else, I tell you." Which, of course is southwestern speak for *it's awful.* "But you were insistent. Anything for the ladies, am I right, Tony?" He slapped Tony on the back.

Now it was Tony's turn to nod his head and act normal.

"But you were happy to trade your car in for, uh, what were you going to call it?"

"Uh, Ladybug?" she offered.

"That's it. Tony, hey, man, are you okay?"

Tony's face had grown pale.

"I traded my car for that?"

Was that incredulous pain in his voice? Tony looked

as if his favorite football, baseball and basketball teams had all lost at the same time on the last play in the final round.

"Well, not an even trade," Jeff assured them.

That must have been where the two grand had come from.

"You paid me four hundred dollars."

Tony made choking sounds.

"I'm not supposed to tell you this, but you really got a good deal out of us last night." Jeff rubbed at the back of his neck. "My boss raked me over the coals this morning, that's for sure."

More choking sounds.

Jeff dropped the pretense of stress and winked. "Guess last night was your lucky night. You couldn't wait to spend your winnings from the Endeavor."

Hold up, that's the first interesting thing Jeff had said, and it had only taken five minutes of conversation.

"Endeavor?" she promoted.

"The casino at the Oklahoma-Texas border. Of course around here we call it the Win Never. Yep, your lucky night indeed, first the cash and then the car."

And still more choking.

"Jeff, could you bring us a couple of waters? That'd be great," she told him and turned to Tony. Jeff needed to go. Fast.

Tony's eyes squinted against the sun as he stared at his former vehicle. "I built that car. At the center we had to take skills classes to keep us occupied and off the streets. I've worked on that car since I was seventeen. Whenever I had the cash and could buy the spare parts," he told her, not bothering to hide the love and pride and sadness in his voice.

That explained why the roadster was older but so well taken care of. The car wasn't just Tony's sleek baby on four wheels, that smooth machine had probably been his salvation.

So much for his theory that even under the influence of whatever the heck they'd been on last night, they still wouldn't do anything they wouldn't normally do. Clearly he loved his old car and would never have sold it under normal circumstances. And who could blame him? Hayden imagined driving it in California, the top down, the sun on her face and palm trees overhead. She could almost feel the warm wind blowing through her hair. Heaven.

"I must have been out of my mind last night. My car is worth twice as much as that piece of cra—uh, sorry. I know that Ladybug was kind of your thing."

Her stomach tightened. That's right—Ladybug *was* her thing. She'd wanted a car painted like that since she was a little girl and had spotted one in the parking lot of the mall. That's when her grandma taught her the word frivolous.

But last night, Anthony Garcia had made her little-girl dream happen for her. She hadn't even realized that it was still even important to her after all these years.

His actions loomed, humbling and horrifying at the same time. She *would* fix this car swap for him. Fix it right now. "I'll be right back," she told him as she aimed for the office.

"Where are you going?"

"Maybe we left our cell phones in there by accident. Signing paperwork, you know, that kind of thing."

Tony nodded and wandered off in the direction of his car. Probably to spend some last quality time with the classic he no longer owned because of her.

Of course she was ill-equipped to do battle. If she still possessed her phone, right now she'd not only know the full value of Ladybug, but also the trade-in value of Tony's car. Plus a rating for the dealership and on Mr. Salesman-Three-Quarters-Ago Jeff. He met her at the glass door juggling two bottles of water. "Oh, there you are." He greeted her with a smile. He tossed her one of the bottles. "Catch."

Jerk. He'd probably expected her to yelp and drop it, or something equally stupid. But she'd played softball in high school and had no problem making the play.

"Jeff, we'll need to trade Ladybug in for Tony's old car."

The salesman tilted his head back and looked down his nose at her. The corner of his lip turned up in an attempt at a smile that came off more like a sneer. Pretend best-friend mode was officially off. "I've already had two people stop by to take a look at that beauty. Our guys gave it a good polish this morning. Have to tell you, we've already sunk some dough into the car. I can work with you, but I suffered some heat for the deal we made last night, and…"

She could fill in the blanks. "It's going to cost me."

Jeff shrugged. "Have to recoup my losses. Pay the guys in the back for their time. The title paperwork alone is worth hours. The accrued wear and tear."

"Since last night?"

"Plus you've already damaged the car I sold you, lady."

She gasped. "Damaged? How?"

He lifted a superior brow. "The spots. Who's going to buy it the way it is now? It will have to be repainted. I'm actually a little surprised you want to trade it back in after all your plans for it. You were both so happy about that little beauty last night."

Now it was her turn to work the angle. "Would you say, unusually happy?"

"Very," he told her with a nod, warming to the subject.

"So then it wouldn't surprise you to hear that Mr. Garcia and I may have been the victims of a suspicious substance last night? One that clouds judgment and induces short-term memory amnesia. How do we know that we weren't dosed here?"

"Now wait a minute—"

"It's easy to verify. A simple blood test." She'd actually done her fair share of volunteering for various drug trials to make a little extra cash, so she understood labs and test results. His nostrils flared and his air of arrogance dropped off fast.

She patted him on the arm, and delivered a wide smile—pretend best-friend mode on high. "I'm sure you had nothing to do with it, Jeff. And I know you wouldn't want there to be any rumors that the dealership made this situation even worse for us. You know how cruel social media can be." Hayden shuddered. "I can only imagine the snarky memes, hashtags and reviews headed your way."

"Well, I…uh…"

Then Jeff straightened and that cocky, overly confident grin returned, and her stomach tightened. Of course, getting the best of him wouldn't be that easy. She was an amateur when it came to manipulation. So she gave him a conspiratorial wink and tried another tactic instead, "Jeff, what's it going to take to get us back in that car today?"

TONY RUBBED AT a nonexistent smudge on the hood of his old car. He'd been nursing this sweet thing back to health since he'd found it missing a fender and ready for the crusher at a salvage yard nine years ago. He'd been searching for spare parts for a shop project at the center, never suspecting he'd stumble onto an endeavor that would consume him and save him at the same time.

He'd wrangled a deal with the guy at the wrecker— he could have the car if he promised to work there every day after school and on Saturdays for five weeks, ringing sales and pulling parts off junkers in the yard.

It had taken another two weeks of work to afford the new parts he'd need to repair his new car and another month to score enough cash for a paint job. Navy hadn't been his first choice—the rebellious teen in him wanted something black with flames down the sides— but the dark blue had been on a closeout sale, and he'd never looked back.

Until now. His car had got him through high school. It had been his crash pad when he'd put all his money into financing his first film and couldn't afford the rent. Been with him on every film since.

And last night he'd given it all up.

A breeze, or maybe it was hot, sexual awareness drifted over his skin. He looked up and there was Hayden, filling his vision. Her long, dark hair bounced around her shoulders as she hurried toward him. Her fit, lightly tanned legs snagged his gaze for a moment. He'd always been a leg man. Short or long or lean—none of that mattered. A woman's leg, from the sexy curve of her calf to the softness of her thighs, always drew his eyes for a second glance.

Yet, he was also entranced by the way her hair framed the roundness of her face, caressing her cheeks the way his fingers wanted to. And by the way her soft lips invited him to take a long, sweet taste… Then there was the sway and rock of her hips as she raced toward him that made his hands itch to curl his fingers around the curve of her waist and slam her against his body to cradle his cock. Oh, hell. He wasn't a leg man after all. *Everything* about Hayden turned him on.

"I see my fate." He tamped down the thought. Forced it from his mind. Because the idea of a woman he barely knew being it for him was ridiculous. No, what he wanted was last night again. Hayden naked. In his arms. Wanting him.

Her breasts lifted and bounced with every step as she walked toward him, and he remembered Betty's hasty apology that she didn't have a bra in Hayden's size. Her nipples poked against the thin cotton of her borrowed T-shirt, and his mouth watered. Last night he would have laved her breasts with his tongue, drawn them into his mouth and teased the tips with his teeth. And he didn't remember one thin detail.

"Here," she called, and she tossed him a set of keys. He caught them one-handed and then glanced down at the key resting in his palm. He'd recognize the shape and cut anywhere. The one thing he'd held on to since he was seventeen. The key to his car.

"How did you…?"

A flirtatious smile curved her lips as she leaned toward him. "Grab the cash out of the glove box of Ladybug and let's go."

She didn't have to tell him twice. In less than two minutes, she was beside him and Ladybug was in the rearview mirror.

"Hayden—" he began after a few minutes of driving together in silence.

"Does the top come down on this car?" she asked.

"Of course."

"Then do it. Today I want to be the woman who rides with the top down and the wind in my hair."

He took his foot off the gas and pulled over to the side of the road so he could lower the top as she wished.

That's when he realized how it had happened. How he'd traded in his car, how he'd painted big black spots on an ugly cheap car, probably how he'd finished his evening in the cabin with a hot tub—because Hayden had wished it.

"I'm not going to see red-and-blue flashing lights behind me anytime soon, am I? Jeff's not calling the police right now?"

"A little late to be asking the question," she told him, then shook her head with a laugh.

She lifted her hips off the seat and Tony was glad he wasn't driving; they'd have wound up in a ditch. Hayden reached into her back pocket and pulled out a folded piece of paper. "All legal. Your car is yours again. Fair and square. Shall I put the paperwork in the glove box?"

He nodded, reaching over to gently tug it open with the knob. His knuckles brushed the supple skin above her knee. Soft and warm. *More, more, more*, his body demanded.

He cleared his throat. "Oh, I found a necklace underneath the cash," he said, handing her a gold chain with a key suspended on it like a pendant.

"I can't believe it, Tony. I've never talked to another person like that in my life," she said as she slipped the chain around her neck and slid it beneath her T-shirt.

"Who?" That soft Texas lilt of hers intoxicated him. His eyes followed the movement of her mouth as she spoke. He ached to trace the outline with his tongue. To suck her full lower lip into his mouth.

"Jeff. There was something so superior about him. Like he knew he'd gotten one over on us last night, and was not so secretly laughing about it. About us."

After stashing the paperwork in the glove box she reached for his hand, threading her fingers through his. Her green eyes caught his, and there was no way in hell he could look anywhere else. Or would want to.

"I knew you'd made Ladybug happen for me last night. I had to make it right for you today."

No one had ever done anything for him. He wouldn't

allow them to. They either quickly moved onto some other hard-luck case, or they held it over his head, waiting to drop the guilt bomb, like his mother. *After all the things I've done for you...*

But somehow Hayden had sneaked her help right in with her laugh and open smile. And she wanted nothing in return.

His throat tightened and he fisted his hands. Then Tony reached for her. He wrapped his fingers around her arms and drew her to him. Her lips were just as soft and full as he'd fantasized moments ago, as he must have sampled over and over again last night. Now they parted as his tongue found their seam, and Hayden moaned when he slid his tongue along hers.

That moan went straight to his cock, making him hard. Making him want things he had no business wanting. He stroked the backs of his fingers across her soft cheek. So smooth. So tantalizing. Then he fisted her hair around his hands, the tendrils curling and ticking his skin. Hayden pressed herself against him, the oh-so-slight brush of her nipples against his chest making him crazy. Only the stupid gearshift kept him from dragging her into his lap.

More.

Had she moaned that? Had he? Hell yes, he wanted more. So much more. Everything.

A car honked loudly as it passed. Tony forced his eyes open as a truck full of teenagers laughed and waved as they sped away.

Hayden's fingers wrapped around his shoulders. Was

she trying to decide whether to push him away from her or tug him closer?

With a deep sigh she leveraged some distance between them, slumping against her seat and fighting for breath.

He found it difficult to drag in air, too. He wrapped his fingers around the steering wheel, commanding his body to settle. But despite the pain he knew he'd be feeling on the drive back to Dallas, he had to chuckle. "Guess I was right earlier."

"When?" she asked, her voice tight.

"When I said that you feel it, too."

4

ABOUT TEN MILES away from the Oklahoma-Texas border, large flashy billboards advertising the Endeavor started popping up along the highway.

Get Lucky—at Endeavor Casino.

Great, now Hayden was thinking about how close she'd come to getting lucky in the car with Tony. Again. The man could kiss.

Perspiration broke out along her forehead and across the back of her neck. Her eyes began to drift shut as her body relived the delicious sensation of his mouth against hers, the taste of his tongue and the heady scent of his skin.

Go All the Way—at Endeavor Casino.

Hayden crossed her legs to stop more sex thoughts. She'd wanted to go all the way with the gorgeous man beside her, that's for sure.

Score Big—at Endeavor Casino.

"Oh, come on!" Tony muttered beside her.

She giggled. "Glad to know I'm not the only one reading nothing but innuendo on these signs."

"Are these ads nothing but insinuation and allusions to sex or am I only seeing it now because I'm frustrated as hell?"

Frustrated? Her stomach did a flip-flop. That Tony could want her even a fraction as much as she wanted to tear off that stupid T-shirt he wore made her mouth dry and her heart beat like crazy.

Was there a hotel at this casino?

She gave her heated cheeks a quick, and hopefully discreet, fanning. "Jeff said if we missed the place then we just weren't looking. Now I understand what he meant. I'm surprised there's no Get It On—at Endeavor Casino," she said. Two could play the covering-awkward-moments-with-humor game.

"Or Do It Big—at Endeavor Casino," he added.

"We should suggest these to their marketing team. Or we could talk about what happened between us a few moments ago."

The traffic grew heavier the closer they came to the Endeavor. Tony flipped on the blinker at the Turn Now to Score sign.

She rubbed her sweaty palms down her legs. "Tony, I—"

But what was there to say? There was a song about this, about just meeting someone and it being crazy. When she'd first heard the song, she'd laughed off the sentiment. You didn't see someone and instantly want him. You had to have shared interests. Common jokes. Complementary outlooks on life.

But with Tony it had been more like: You. Me. Bed. How do you talk about that rationally? With the person you were so completely irrational about?

Parking was free—the last thing that would be, Hayden was sure. Tony pulled into a space and shut off the car. He turned in the seat, his dark eyes sparking with exactly what she wanted to see—need and want for her. Completely irrational.

"Or we could get some answers from the casino and talk about us later."

She couldn't nod fast enough. Apparently Tony liked to play the avoidance game, as well.

What had happened to roll with it? She'd tossed it to the side at the first hint of real introspection. "Absolutely let's put that off."

"For as long as possible. Agreed."

She'd also ignore the fact that they'd just found they shared a complementary outlook on life—even if it was filled with avoidance and most likely dysfunction.

Hayden reached for the door handle, but Tony clasped her arm. Gently. The pads of his fingers lightly caressed her skin, as if he couldn't help himself. She twisted in her seat to ask what he needed. Then his lips were warm and insistent on her mouth. Her. That's what he'd needed. Her.

Delight and pleasure engulfed her. It took her a moment to respond since he'd caught her so off guard, but only a moment. She opened her lips to him and their tongues entwined as she threw her hands around his neck.

He jerked away from her.

"That was really getting interesting," she protested, her eyes still closed and her breathing thready.

He laughed, a sensual chuckle deep in his throat that she craved to hear again and again. "Too interesting. You bring out something in me, especially in cars." He straightened. "Let's get our answers."

Because then they could start asking new questions.

He grabbed her hand as they wound their way through the parking lot. How many times had he taken her hand today? Such a simple gesture, and yet she really enjoyed it. Her last couple of boyfriends had been just as studious as she was and spent as much time either at work or in the lab as she had, so there hadn't been a lot of time for the pleasure of merely touching of hands. But she liked it. More than liked it. The gesture was intimate and personal. She better be careful, or she'd be drifting into shared interests territory. This was supposed to be Project Getting To Know The Man You Plan To Romp On Later, not Project Overanalyze Every Gesture So You Will Fall In Love.

The dings and electronic whistles of the slot machines greeted them along with a haze of cigarette smoke and flashing lights as they stepped inside the Endeavor. The casino designers had apparently adopted an overcoming-every-obstacle theme with salutes to space exploration, holograms depicting crossing a raging sea and a bizarre display with electricity. Well, she was about to endeavor to learn all she could.

"Hey, Hay," called a woman in a sky-blue strappy cocktail dress as she rushed toward them.

Tony choked back a laugh.

She shot him some shade, which was difficult in the dimly lit room, but he only shrugged. "You have to admit the nickname's kind of catchy."

"I admit nothing."

"Come to hit the tables again?" the woman asked once she neared them.

Hayden shook her head. "Oh, I don't know how to play blackjack."

The waitress gave her shoulder a playful shove. "Ha, ha, that's not how it looked here yesterday. And thanks again for the nice tip last night, especially since the two of you were only drinking water." She gave her another playful elbowing. "Of course, you were already flying pretty high by the time you got here."

Hayden's ears perked up like a puppy who hears the sound of the treat bag opening. *Flying high? Before?* A new clue. Okay, so they'd already been under the influence of whatever the heck they'd been subjected to when they'd arrived at the Endeavor.

"Trying your luck again?"

"Something like that," Tony told her.

She shot Hayden a conspiratorial wink. "I'm sure you got pretty lucky last night. The two of you, whew—" She fanned herself with the drink tray, the makeshift breeze ruffling the curling tendrils of hair that had escaped from her bun.

Now normally—if this kind of situation were normal—Hayden would be mortified right about now. *Get a room* was a motto she lived by, and now people had witnessed her lusty intentions toward Tony?

But then, she was at a casino where a fresco of a

naked Prometheus stealing fire and gifting it to mortals stretched above her head. Their friendly cocktail waitress had probably seen way weirder stuff play out here on the floor.

"I think Danny is dealing again. He was bummed when you two hit it out of here so quickly. He's saving for school and that tip you gave him was a decent little start. It's wonderful when nice people win."

"Maybe you should go over there and see him, Tony," Hayden told him with a smile. Of course he'd have to figure out who Danny was, but Hayden didn't feel one tiny bit sorry since he'd played the same trick on her at the car dealership. It was going to be fun watching him try to bluff his way out of this one.

"Sure, and you could—"

"Oh, I know what she can do. They just posted your picture to the Wall of Winners. Follow me. I'll show you where it is."

So she didn't get to watch Tony scramble to come up with a story for Danny, but he didn't get to weasel his way out of it, either. After a quick finger wave, Hayden dutifully followed the waitress over to the wall.

"These pictures only stay up until the end of the year, so if you want the photo afterward, the manager can mail it to you. He does that a lot. Goodwill and all."

Hayden finally managed to snag a discreet glance at her name tag—Darcy.

Near one of the complimentary drink stands was a large gold and glittery wall with black-and-white photos attached. Dozens of pictures of people, all smiling, stared out at her. Then she spotted her snapshot. She wore the clothes she'd been dressed in Thursday morning before she'd gone to school and then work—one of the last things she remembered. Why'd she have to pick that morning to wear her favorite bra? Still mourning.

Beside her in the photo stood Tony, looking so handsome in jeans and a dark shirt with his sleeves carelessly rolled up to his elbows. He'd draped his arm around her shoulders and her hip grazed his. They appeared so at ease with one another. Intimate. Definitely a couple.

Although she had been gazing solely at the camera with a wide, easy smile on her face, the photographer had caught Tony midglance. At her. As if he couldn't force his eyes away. When had a man ever looked at her like that? Warmth spread through her body and some place in her chest began to ache. She had known then how it felt to have a man shoot you that longing, I-want-only-you kind of look. But now she didn't. She longed to have him fix on her again like that.

"Why can't I remember?" she groaned.

"Excuse me," Darcy said.

She shook her head, "Oh, it's nothing. At least nothing a time machine couldn't fix."

"Or a Time Lord. Gotta go. Someone's signaling for a drink."

Alone, Hayden studied the photo, searching for a clue as to how they'd wound up here at the Endeavor. But her gaze kept drifting to Tony. How many times had she slid her fingers through his dark hair? She'd probably run her palms down his chest and over his flat abs half a dozen times. She certainly wanted to now, and last night she'd have had the freedom. She stared at his mouth. Hayden could only imagine how many times she'd trailed her lips across his mouth, down his skin, grazed his nipples with her teeth when she'd been allowed free rein to his entire delicious body.

She sucked in a breath and closed her eyes, ordering her thoughts to stay focused and her hormones to stay tamped down. C'mon, wasn't as if she'd never been a teenager. And they had to solve this mystery if she had any hope of being sure there was no danger to the future she'd worked so hard for.

Lean fingers settled on her shoulders and gifted her with a gentle but way-too-short massage. She breathed in Tony's addictive scent and the warmth returned. She relaxed against the solidness of his chest. "That isn't fair," she told him, half moaning the words.

"Huh?"

She'd been trying to talk herself out of not responding to him until they solved the mystery, and here he was touching her. Making her body warm and soften toward him. Welcome him. She was more ramped up than ever. Why was she resisting him again?

"Oh, what the hell." She smoothed her hair out of his way and leaned farther into his tender fingers. "More," she urged, her voice low.

"You look tense."

She was a lot of things. Hot. Turned on. Aching for his touch. So yeah, she'd accept tense. With a sigh the muscles of her shoulders relaxed under the kneading of his fingers.

"I can't keep this up," he told her after a moment.

"You only need to continue until I'm done."

His chest rumbled against her back. "You can't mean what I think you mean."

She faced him and gave Tony a wink. "Maybe." Although technically she'd only been thinking of him massaging her until he'd worked out the knot under her shoulder blade.

The smile faded from Tony's face, and something dark and sensual flickered to life in his eyes. And he was looking at her. Just as he had in the picture. Her skin tingled in response, her breasts became heavy inside the thin cami.

Amazing. That's how it felt to have a man look at her like this. As if he'd crawl on broken and bloody hands for a touch. A taste.

Her cheeks heated. She'd drag his mouth down to hers, grip him by the wrists and shove his hands on her breasts if she didn't wrest her gaze from his. Right. Now.

"Hayden, I—"

Hayden twisted away from him, then squinted at the picture as something she hadn't noticed before caught her attention. Maybe it was because she was hyperaware. Or maybe she frantically needed a distraction to make her think of something other than sex. Whatever it was, she now zeroed in on an object in the photo she didn't recognize. "What's on my wrist?"

Tony rubbed the back of his neck. For a moment she *felt* the pressure of his gaze as he studied her profile. She tried to act naturally, as if having the hottest man she'd ever seen devour her with his eyes was something she was used to. Yeah, sure, that happened in the engineering lab all the time. He stood so close she felt the muscles of his arms tense. As if he was getting ready to grab her. To drag her against his chest. Hold her close. But then he exhaled and focused all that intense energy where she'd pointed.

He peered at their image. "Those are wristbands we're wearing, aren't they?"

She nodded. "I think so. The half paper, half plastic kind you get at dance clubs."

"So I either picked you up there or—"

She held up both hands. "Whoa, whoa, I may have picked you up, for all we know."

"And I would have let you." Then his brow furrowed. "Strange, nightclubs aren't usually my thing."

"The only time I'm at a club is to work."

He lifted a brow. "I didn't think it was possible after you threw out the whole you-picking-me-up scenario, but this conversation just got a lot more interesting."

"I work at a club waiting tables occasionally. I don't strip. The more I think about it the more I doubt I picked you up."

He held up a hand. "Don't ruin it for me."

"Ha, ha—I'm saying we must have gone to the club together. You said clubbing's not your scene—it's not mine, either. Believe me when I tell you, nothing turns you off drinking and being rowdy more than serving beer and potato skins to people drinking and being rowdy."

"So this club had to have offered something pretty special to make us go inside. Sounds like a clue. Good work."

Darcy walked by, her tray empty. "Darcy, you wouldn't happen to know if any cell phones have been turned in?" Hayden asked.

"We have a lost and found. It's right by the boutique. Let me go drop this order in the kitchen and I'll show you the way."

Hayden tensed when she was alone again with Tony. Her attraction to him was just too sudden. Too intense. Her last two boyfriends had been lab partners. They'd been slowly deepening relationships that had grown out of friendships. Not this instant heat. Instant want. Some space to clear her thoughts wouldn't be a bad thing right about now.

"Everyone is so nice to us here," she tossed out for something to say. "I'm surprised they even remember who we are. They must have thousands of people parade through here every day."

"When you're giving away Benjamins…" Tony joked.

But she didn't get the joke. "Benjamins?"

"Benjamins are hundred-dollar bills. At least that's what all the hip kids call them. When I finally found Danny, he mentioned the kind of money we were spreading around."

Hayden laughed. "I was raised by my grandparents and I wanted to be an engineer. Believe me, math girl here was never hip. Come to think of it, Darcy mentioned that we gave the staff good tips, but I had no idea she was talking that kind of money. I don't even want to tell you what my college student loan looks like right now. There's no way I'd be passing out the Benjis. Not even Lincolns. Maybe a George Washington here and there."

Ugh, she was rambling. *Stop referring to money by its president—you sound like an amateur.* But had she lost her damn mind last night? One Ben—just one single hundred-dollar bill would keep her in tuna, noodles and dry cereal for a month.

She glowered at her image in the photo. Last-night Hayden had a large smile, a wristband and yes, cash wadded in her hands. "How much did we make last night?"

"Just a hair less than what we'd need to catch the attention of the IRS agent, according to Danny."

"Ready, you guys?" Darcy asked, and they dutifully followed her as she meandered a weaving path through the various tables. A path designed to take them past every means of gambling, from roulette, blackjack and Texas Hold 'Em to the row after row of dinging, clanging and flashing slot machines.

Beside the cages stood a lone unbarred desk with an Information sign suspended from the ceiling above a team member's head. Darcy waved to the guy at the desk. "These two are looking for some cell phones."

He shook his head. "Sorry, folks, cells are rarely turned in because they can be easily pawned. But you're welcome to check." He bent down and retrieved a large plastic tub from under the desk. Several jackets, a ball cap and, oddly, a lone shoe rested on top of a large heap.

"You mind if I dump this out? It would be easier to sift through," Hayden asked.

He shrugged. "Be my guest."

She tipped the large bin over, catching the pyramid of clothes before they toppled off the desk. But something jangled and tumbled out of the pile, clanged against the desk, then dropped. Hayden gasped as she spotted the bright green unicorn horn against the beige of the carpet.

"My keys." Hayden stooped to grab them, closing her fingers tightly around the beauty that was her apartment, mailbox and car keys.

Her throat tightened. She hadn't realized how much she needed this tiny bit of normalcy. Something concrete and solid and not full of mystery. For the first time since waking up with a strange man in a strange place and driving a strange car, she felt as if all of this might just work out. They'd find their phones and her car and learn just what the heck had happened to them last night.

With a relieved sigh she reached up, wrapped her fingers behind Tony's neck, stood up on tiptoe and kissed him quick on his closed lips before he had a chance to respond.

"C'mon. There's a little boutique over there, I'm going to buy you some jeans."

"Wow. That's not what I was expecting."

She threw him a faux haughty smirk. "I know how to treat a man."

Feeling light and carefree, she raced toward the boutique, daring him to follow.

The mannequins posed behind the glass display windows were dressed in everything from Endeavor T-shirts and trendy skirts to expensive leather jackets.

Muted music lilted in the store and the glaring sounds of machines and haze of cigarette smoke faded as they entered.

Although small, the boutique didn't waste its real estate on clothing sporting prices with anything less than three digits—in front of the decimal. On her budget, she usually shopped at thrift stores and purchased her jeans at the feed supply store, but tonight she was going to get one of the designer pair with the rhinestones on the pockets that the girls wore on campus.

Hayden grabbed one in what she hoped was her size. Then she plucked a white knit blouse off the rack. It was fitted with sleeves that ended right at the elbow. She'd be stuck with the cami, though—no bras or panties in sight. The attendant looked up long enough to direct Hayden to a tiny dressing room in the corner, then returned to texting on her phone.

She grabbed a pair of jeans she thought would fit Tony nicely. With a quick tug, Hayden pulled the curtain closed and quickly shucked her shorts to slip on the soft, very expensive denim. She twisted to check for fit—nice and snug—and then sat to make sure she could still breathe if she sat down. So far, so good. Now for the final test. The mirror inside the dressing room was just a halfsie, but a full-length mirror was affixed to a wall outside the dressing room. Hayden ducked out of the change room and went over to the mirror. She turned so she could spy her backside. "Wow, expensive jeans really do make your butt look—"

"Amazing," Tony said, and she met his gaze in the mirror. So he liked the shape of her ass. Great, because she liked the shape of his everything. Where was Darcy with that drink tray so she could fan herself? "I'm just going to, uh, try on a new shirt," she managed to stammer.

She fled into the safety of the dressing room. Took two deep breaths, and then gave her reflection a rueful grin. These jeans were trouble for sure.

She reached for the hem of her shirt and tugged the T-shirt up and over her head, but it got caught. "Ouch."

"You okay in there?" Tony asked.

Hayden tugged again on the material and another sharp pain ran along her scalp. She tried to lower her T-shirt, but the action only brought more pain. She was stuck. "There's something caught in my hair, and I can't see how to get it out," she whispered.

"Do you want me to come in and help?"

Her smile widened at his hopeful tone.

"Yes, but be discreet about it," she whispered back.

Tony pushed away the privacy curtain and joined her, then pulled the curtain back into place. Shielding them. He stood beside her, big and handsome, and the dressing room suddenly shrank. "Don't worry, the woman at the register is too busy playing Candy Crush Saga to notice what we're doing."

She felt his fingers gently probe her scalp. Ugh, she could imagine how stupid she looked. Cami and T-shirt almost over her head, her stomach bare. The new jeans the only bright spot.

"Okay, your hair and part of the strap of your cami have tangled around the cuts of the key. Let me just…" With a few careful tugs and pulls, she was free and the tension in her scalp eased. "I'll help you with the shirt," he told her and whisked the material the rest of the way off her body.

And like that she was topless. With a soft gasp she turned her back to him, only to realize she now faced the mirror. She quickly covered her breasts.

His wide-eyed gaze met hers in the reflective glass. "I'm sorry, Hayden. I forgot…" His words trailed off as she licked her dry lips. His eyes narrowed and she felt him stiffen behind her.

Her blood pounded in her veins and she found it hard to breathe. Naked desire and hunger waged in the darkness of his eyes. He wanted her, and the knowledge of that want made her knees shaky. Naked thrills shot through her body and pooled in her stomach. He wanted her and she wanted him. It was as simple as that.

She swallowed and slowly lowered her hands.

His quick intake of breath at her actions excited her. Electrified her. All the tiny hairs on her arms and the back of her neck stood up. She watched in the mirror as his gaze lowered and settled on her bare breasts. Her nipples hardened under the intensity of his eyes.

Of course the lighting in the room just had to be fluorescent. Ugh. But Tony didn't seem to mind the way the light played along the curves of her skin and the darkness of her nipples.

"Touch me," she urged.

Her eyes fell closed as he cupped her breasts.

"No, Hayden, watch me stroke your skin." His voice was low and hoarse and a whole new set of thrills coursed along her nerve endings.

She lifted her gaze and met his in the mirror. Hayden followed his fingers as they circled her nipples and drew them tight and achy and needy.

"You have beautiful breasts," he whispered against her temple, and she watched and felt him lick the shell of her ear. How could something that was fairly tame make her whole body tremble?

"You like this, don't you? Knowing only a thin layer of fabric separates us from being caught? It excites you."

It hadn't until he'd mentioned it. Probably would never again, but something about now…this moment…

"I want you to watch as I make you come," he whispered, his breath a caress against her sensitized skin.

She nodded, wanting that, too. Needing it. Hayden had never ached for anything more.

His right hand trailed lower and splayed against her stomach. "Follow my fingers with your eyes. Don't look away." His hand drifted to the waistband of her jeans, and moisture pooled between her legs. She was ready. So ready.

"How are those jeans working out?" the attendant called.

Now? She chose right then to suddenly begin caring about her job?

"You have to answer her," Tony said, desire lacing his words.

She took a calming breath that hopefully made her voice sound normal. "Nice," she finally managed to get out between gritted teeth. The corner of Tony's mouth curved in a satisfied smile. She turned in his arms, breaking the erotic connection.

"Proud of yourself, are you?" she asked him.

He kissed the tip of her nose, a surprisingly intimate and calming gesture. "I would be if my cock wasn't about to explode. You sure know how to pick your moments," he told her on a groan. He wrapped his arms around her and pulled her against his chest.

"*I* picked the moment? You were the one who came in here," she reminded him, the aching desire settling down to a banked wanting.

"Who invited whom?" he protested, and she giggled against the muscled hardness of his body.

After a moment, she left his embrace and stooped to pick up her cami. Tony made a noise as she settled the material over her breasts then covered up further with the shirt from the rack.

And all the time he stood watching her.

"I grabbed a pair of jeans for you," she said, nodding toward the neatly folded denim on the bench inside the dressing room. "Why don't you try them on so we can get out of here," she teased.

"Maybe the woman who left a mound of lost and found clothes piled high shouldn't be giving orders," he teased right back.

Her smile instantly vanished. How many times had she been left to clean up after someone who should have known better? She'd worked many waitressing and catering jobs to put her through school, and one thing she'd learned was that a lot of rich people didn't have the manners to match their money. And now she was one of them. "Oh, no. I'll be right back."

But Tony shook his head. "No worries, I took care of it. I also gave him a—"

"You don't have to say it. You gave him a Benjamin."

He winked again and she tried to stealthily escape from the dressing room. She tried not to imagine him stripping off his shorts, but she got all hot and tingly, anyway.

A few moments later Tony emerged, appearing more like the Anthony Garcia in the picture on the winners wall. Jeans, a casual cotton button-down and rolled-up sleeves. How could he make such simple clothing look so effortlessly sexy? She couldn't even kid herself— the man would make overalls hot. And that was damn near impossible.

"If your keys were here, maybe your car is, too."

"Why didn't I think of that?" Probably because she'd been too distracted with thoughts of kissing Tony. Thoughts of Tony in ass-hugging jeans. And thoughts of Tony's hands on her body.

After paying for their clothes, they raced back to Tony's car and did a slow, lane-by-lane inspection of the parking lot, searching for her car.

"Nothing." Her shoulders drooped after they rounded onto the last lane.

He gave her hand a light squeeze. "Your car being here was a long shot anyway."

Hayden raised a brow. "Oh?"

"What are we, an hour, an hour and a half away from Texas? In that picture we were obviously together, so what are the chances we would have driven two cars here?"

Her clunker wasn't much good for anything other than getting her to work and to school, and it certainly wasn't up to a cross-border road trip. "You're right. I wouldn't have wanted to take my car all this way."

"So we try to figure out what club we were at and go from there."

"Guess we have a new plan." Five minutes later they were back on the highway. "Goodbye, Endeavor. Thanks for all the cash."

"I wonder why we stopped there anyway."

"Probably my idea. Along with never having been to Oklahoma, I've never been to a casino, either. My grandparents frowned on gambling so it never really interested me, but ever since that movie came out about those engineering and math students at MIT making big bucks at blackjack my friends have egged me on."

"You think we were counting cards last night?"

Hayden shook her head. "Believe me, when you have as many student loans as I do, it was something I researched. But the casinos are too good at spotting it now. Too many safety measures. Last night was just a lot of luck, I'm sure."

"Seems to be the story of my life since last night."

"You're forgetting the skunk," she reminded him.

"Since I don't remember the incident, I guess it doesn't count."

"Just like the se—" Whoa. Had she almost brought up the sex they must have enjoyed last night? Her hands fisted at her sides. Maybe he hadn't noticed.

"The what? Were you about to mention the sex?"

She folded her arms against her chest. "Never mind. I thought we agreed to put off talking about that subject."

"True, but that was before you flashed me in the dressing room. Besides, if a woman wants to talk sex, it's my duty as a gentleman to indulge her. It's the right thing to do."

Tiny shivers erupted and feathered down her back. Oh, she could imagine Tony indulging her all right. And all the clues pointed to one long evening of his doing just that. She'd never been to Oklahoma—boom, road trip. Casino on her bucket list—crossed off. Ladybug car? Heck, she hadn't thought of that little interest since she was ten, and yet, he'd made it happen last night. All clues pointed to Tony spoiling her between the sheets, too. Slow, unhurried kisses. Soft, full-body strokes. *Dependable orgasms.*

She cleared her throat. "So before we spotted this car, you were telling me how you went from juvie to filmmaker."

He didn't say anything for a moment. Had he noticed the rapidness of her breathing? The way her skin must be flushed? The tenseness of her muscles?

"Had I gotten as far as the Transitional Center?" he finally asked.

"You mentioned it, but I'm still not clear on what it is."

"Basically a last chance. Twelve guys, all of us in high school, lived at the center. It was kind of like a dorm, I'd imagine. I shared a bedroom with another boy. There was a communal bathroom down the hall and a kitchen by the director's housing area. We all had to take a night cooking dinner. First home where I had to do chores, too," he told her with a laugh, thinking of the memory with obvious fondness. "We'd go to school during the day. No getting out of that. And at night, we'd work or learn a trade. They kept us so busy we couldn't get into trouble. Grade checks, attendance checks, room checks, if there was a way to track us, it was done."

"And that's where you learned to fix cars," she filled in for him. "Did you want to be a mechanic?"

"Yeah, I liked the work. No surprises with cars. They run or they don't. You figure out what's broken and you get the part and you make the car work again. People aren't like that."

Was he talking about his mother? Other guys at the center? Or maybe himself? "So how did you get into film?"

"The center received a lot of donations. From churches and scout groups, that kind of thing. One night, it was my turn to sort through the boxes. I tried to trade my shift with everyone. No takers. It had been raining for three days straight. I know no one wants to hear people from Southern California whine about rain, but we'd been stuck inside and I was itching to patrol scrap yards for car parts. The last thing I wanted to do was be stuck inside going through shirts and pants and stuff for the kitchen.

"But in one of the boxes I found a video camera. I tinkered around with it for a bit and got it to work. After that, I filmed everything—what happened at school, at work and in the center. It didn't matter if it was interesting or not.

"My senior year of high school I signed up for an AV class, and the teacher let me use the editing equipment after school. The teacher showed the film I put together that year for the senior banquet."

She couldn't help but smile hearing the pride and gratification in his words, and she realized it was the first time he must have felt those things. Although all her family was gone now, she'd always known they were behind her 100 percent. They'd shared in the delight of her accomplishments and encouraged her when she felt down or stumbled in her quest to go to college and become an engineer. Behind Tony's playful smile and teasing attitude loomed a lot of pain.

"I had caught the film bug, and I knew the story I wanted to tell first," he said, his fingers once again drumming on the steering wheel. "I wanted to make a documentary about kids growing up on the street. Like me. I was lucky. If I hadn't caught some big breaks, I'd be in jail right now. Or worse. Still, it was a lot of sleeping in my car and scrounging up money so I could rent some studio time to cut and edit my film. I had to learn everything at the library—distribution networks, how to get involved in film festivals and streaming sites."

"How many documentaries have you made now?"

"Seven, but I also return to the subjects from my first film to get an update on how they're doing. And this is the first time I've ever left California—usually I stick to where I grew up."

"And look what happened. You lost your memory and almost lost your car."

He gifted her with a flirty sideways glance. "Hasn't been all bad."

How did he do it? Just a few words and one heated gaze and he had her heartbeat ramped up and cheeks feeling hot.

"Thank you for sharing your story, Tony. With most guys you have to pry personal details out of them with a crowbar and fire-retardant tongs."

"We already covered this—you should date better men."

Enough with the sexy banter. It was time to play her cards. "Are you volunteering?"

5

"THOUGHT I VOLUNTEERED last night."

Checkmate. Okay she was mixing up her metaphors, but whoa, his statement floored her. Because somewhere in her mind a thought taunted her—although he didn't have any memory of last night, he did regret waking up with her this morning. Some tiny prickling doubt had warned her that he'd ditch her quick—just as soon as they knew the truth.

He'd dashed all her self-doubts and assumptions with one sentence. Talk about laying your cards on the table. Now *that* was the correct metaphor. A tingly excited warmth settled in the small of her back.

He rubbed at his chin. There'd been no razor in the cabin and she spotted the beginnings of his delightful dark stubble.

"This is crazy for me, too," he said. "I've never done a one-night stand, and I doubt I would have started last night. Not my bag. I think I met you last night and there was no way in hell I wanted to say goodbye. Today, all this time on the road with you, hasn't changed that."

The breath whooshed out of her body. Up until a few moments ago, Hayden would have been able to write this whole disastrous weekend off as an adventure. In the future she'd be able to recall it as a pleasant memory of a couple of nights with a hot guy she'd met. But now she would never be able to do that. Tony had just made it all real.

She had to be real in return. She owed him that. She fidgeted with her hands for a moment, then shook off her nerves. "Well, if you're still volunteering, I'd like that."

He glanced her way and flashed her a sexy smile that she felt all the way to her toes. Hayden smiled back, and even though she knew it had to be all kinds of goofy, she just didn't care. She had a date with a hot guy.

They chatted and drove for another forty-five miles, but finally Hayden could no longer ignore that breakfast had been several long hours ago. "I hate to say this, since we're trying to get to Dallas quickly, but I'm really hungry."

"Can't hold out?" he asked.

"I get a little cranky when I haven't eaten," she admitted.

"As cranky as when you don't have coffee in the morning?"

Any man who'd hang around after witnessing non-caffeinated Hayden in her prime was a keeper. "Maybe not that bad, but I still wouldn't push your luck," she shot back.

"No worries. I could fill up the gas tank, too. Sandwiches okay? I saw a sign for a diner."

"Works for me."

They found the diner nestled between bay after bay of gas pumps for both cars and 18-wheelers. A true truck stop; Hayden was delighted. All kinds of knick-knacks were for sale inside the gift shop, from shot glasses, T-shirts and silly magnetic signs the purchaser could attach to their car.

"If they'd sold ladybug spots, we could have saved ourselves a whole lot of hassle," he teased.

Inside the diner, a sign invited them to seat themselves and they found a booth of worn turquoise vinyl in a corner. "This is just the kind of place my grandparents avoided," she confessed as she reached for one of the plastic menus on the table.

"We can go somewhere else."

She shook her head quickly. "No, this is great. Growing up, we didn't have a lot of money for meals out. My grandparents believed if you were going to the expense of eating in a restaurant, it should be an experience. So they avoided fast-food joints and greasy spoons. They loved taking me out for different kinds of food. I was the only one in the fifth grade who knew what foie gras and couscous was. It wasn't until college that I realized there was a whole new way to eat."

"The perfect truck-stop diner food is chili and grilled cheese," he suggested as their waitress approached.

Hayden folded her menu and replaced it inside the metal clip on their booth. "I'll have that."

It wasn't until after their waitress scribbled their

order on a notepad and raced away that Hayden realized they'd been spending money as if they had a
green bill gifting tree in the backyard. Tony had slept
in his car to finance his films, and here she was blowing cash on designer jeans. But he didn't seem to be
doing so bad now.

"After your first film, was it easier to get studio time
and supplies?" she asked, though it was still tough to
meet his eyes.

The waitress set down two plastic glasses of iced tea.
"Your food should be out in a minute."

"Thanks." He smiled at the waitress, and the older
woman shot her a look saying, *honey, you done good.*

And maybe tonight she'd do even better.

He nodded. "It got easier, and a lot more doors
opened after the film was nominated."

"Nominated?" The man had been an open book,
willing to share his secrets, and now she couldn't get
two sentences out of him.

He rubbed at his chin, and then busied his hands
peeling off the paper casing from a straw. "For an Academy Award. You hear this all the time, but it really was
an honor just to be nominated."

She lifted her hands. "Whoa, hold up. Did you just
say an Academy Award? As in the Oscars?"

He grinned. "I have the tuxedo rental receipt to prove
it."

"Oh, so it's okay to offer up an interesting tidbit of
information now that the big news has been released?"
she kidded. Despite what he'd assured her earlier, she
suspected he still harbored a secret or two. Then she

laughed. "You rented a tux to go to the most important night in film? As if you were Oscar's best man?"

"I thought about buying one, but I'd have had to wear it every day for the next year to justify it. And I remembered not all my ideas are brilliant."

Man, oh man, why did she have to find his self-deprecating humor so damn irresistible? She was actually leaning toward him. Softening. And the closer she got to Texas, the more the real world intruded. She could reconcile herself to a few nights of fun, but things turned dangerous when emotions became involved.

"Actually, it was for the best that I didn't buy the tux because I haven't been nominated since. When you're not trying is when it happens."

Kind of like falling in love.

Finding the right guy.

Desperately trying to slow down time.

Their waitress returned with their food. The grilled cheese was that perfect golden brown that made her stomach rumble. A pile of shredded cheese topped their chili. Granny and Grandpa had missed some of the simple joys in life by saving up and only going after the big ones.

"You can make it up to me," she said. "While our food cools, tell me every little detail. Don't scrimp. I want it all."

"Sunday's not the only celebration. There are all these parties leading up to it, especially the two nights before the actual ceremony. A lot of times that's where the big deals are made, so even though the ballots have long since been calculated and triple-checked, there's still work to do for filmmakers like me. It sounds fun and the glad-handing is important, but it's not the kind of work I want to be doing or really enjoy. I have a lot more stories to tell."

Tony picked up his spoon and began to stir his chili, the cheese melting and becoming stringy. "I reminded myself to be cool. That I was a tough guy. I didn't go to film school, winning an award wasn't my dream. But then I got there and it was impossible not to get caught up in it all. Fans line the streets waiting to catch a glimpse of famous people, but they waved and cheered for me, too."

"Did you walk the red carpet?"

He nodded. "In fact there's two. One for all the really famous people and the press, and another for the rest of the nominees and their guests. But at the entrance the two carpets merge into one and we all walked in together. Backstage the wine flowed nonstop, but they would only let us get up or come back into the theater during commercials. The main thing I remember, because they said it over and over again, was to get upstage quickly, say something inspiring and get offstage even quicker."

"It's a long night," she said, and reached for her sandwich.

"True, although being there, I was never bored. Of course I didn't win, but because I was nominated I'm now in a position that I can make the movies that I want to make. How I want to make them."

"Don't like people telling you what to do, I see."

He laughed. "Would have made life a lot easier if I had."

"Maybe not easier, just different."

"Spoken by someone who's a bit of a stickler for the rules."

She made a scoffing sound. "A bit? More like a serial rule follower. When I'm driving, my hands are always at ten and two. I never stray to the left on a sidewalk and I stress about those plastic tags when I'm buying clothes."

"What's to worry about that?"

"I'm afraid that the person ringing me up will forget to take it off and I'll trigger the warning system and the alarms will go off and someone will think I've shoplifted. Did you see that? I had a full-body shudder at the thought of living through that experience."

"So you being here with me…?" he teased.

Hayden nodded and laughed at the same time. "Yeah, breaking all the rules."

"And how does that feel?"

"Wow, you really can take it from laughing and teasing to full-on serious in a heartbeat."

"You're evading. Is that a tactic that usually works for you?" he asked.

Clearly the man wasn't going to let her get away with not sharing. Damn.

He rapped his knuckles on the table as if he'd just realized something. "You don't like talking about yourself, do you? And especially about feelings, which is classic because you were the one hassling me earlier about men refusing to talk about their emotions."

Hayden shrugged. "Kind of had enough of it when

I was little. When you're in the second grade and both your parents die in an accident, that's all anyone wants you to do. Talk about yourself. Talk about how sad you are. Hayden yelled at another kid for taking her marker. Let's give her a feelings journal. Oh, she doesn't want to play dodgeball? Let's send her to talk with someone. Like no one took it into consideration that dodgeball is the worst game in the world. Who thinks it's a good idea to just line up and wait to be hit with a ball?"

"So I shouldn't take your markers, huh?"

"Damn straight. Can't guarantee I won't yell."

Tony stretched out his hand and gave hers a light squeeze. Nothing long or drawn out, but it was nice. Uplifting rather than comforting. Connecting.

"You don't have that raised-by-the-state look about you," he said, not letting the inquisition end.

"No, my grandparents took me in. How could you tell?"

"You have that…sheltered look about you."

"Great. That's what I was going for. That or stick-in-the-mud."

A smile pulled at the corner of his lip. "No, I mean you don't seem like a person who's afraid to care. That's a good thing, Hayden."

Was that the kind of woman Tony was used to? Had none of the women he'd dated cared for this man?

"My grandparents took me in," she repeated, talking so she could avoid thinking about what it would mean to care for him. She was about to start a new life that meant everything to her. And he was a wanderer.

She'd be in a whole new world of hurt if she let herself fall for him.

"Tell me about your grandparents," he encouraged.

"You can blame the sheltered look on them. They weren't like those former hippies you hear about or see in commercials—they were old school." Her heart warmed at the thought of their dear faces. Now gone, too. "Manners and respect were important to them. So were good grades, being in bed by nine o'clock on a school night and lots and lots of rules."

"So that's where you get your serial rule following."

She nodded. "Yes, I came by it honestly, but don't call me that as if it's a bad thing. I've often heard kids in class saying, 'don't tell me what to do' and 'rules are made to be broken,' which is all well and good a time or two, but you really can't live your life that way. Where does it end? How would we know how to act?"

His eyes narrowed and she couldn't help but smile.

"Take this situation, for example. You and me." And yes, she *would* ignore that quivery sensation that was invading her stomach at the mention of Tony and Hayden as a *we*. "Things would be a lot easier right now if there were a few rules we could follow. It's not like I can search 'waking up with a stranger and no memory' in Google and know what to do with a wikiHow picture explanation."

"But not following the rules is how we got into this situation," he told her, his voice low and his gaze intent. "I'd never want you to regret me."

She sucked in a breath and dropped her gaze.

"You really hate it, don't you? Talking emotions."

"Have you spent a summer in Texas yet?"

Tony shook his head.

"It's really hot. Weeks of triple-digit temps every day. All sun and no shade. Energy-sucking heat blasts you the moment you step out of your car. But for some reason, every retailer or grocery store cranks up the AC to a refrigerator-like temperature, so you walk inside and it's this dueling sensation of intense discomfort and utter relief at the same time. That's how this moment with you feels."

Tony began to laugh and the tenseness of the moment faded.

"So no sleeping in your car anymore?" she asked, changing the subject.

"Only if I want to."

And predictably Hayden's mind conjured up images of her body entwined with his in the backseat of his car. Hot and sweaty, making out like teenagers with no place to go. She couldn't escape the crazy hot pull of attraction. The carnal sensation he aroused in her was heady, electric and nothing she'd ever felt before with a man. She'd be adding "listening to that sexy voice of his" to her Top Ten List of All Time Favorite Things To Do. The scent of him was an assault to her senses. Even just an accidental brush of his warm body against hers made her shiver.

Was he experiencing the same thing? Earlier he'd asked if she felt *it*, too. Boy, did she.

"I keep thinking I should be shocked and worried about all this. I got a tattoo last night. I spent the night with a stranger, but I just can't make myself get worked up about it," she told him as she reached for her spoon. Then she stilled as a jolt of understanding made her pause. "Tony, that's it! What if whatever we were given didn't just take away our memories, but also took away the natural instinct to panic? What if it wiped away our nerves and the fear that holds us back from doing the things we want to do? I woke up in the woods, naked and in bed with a stranger with no memory of how I got there. There are scarier movies based on less. And yet, I never really freaked. I really should have freaked."

His eyes narrowed, but his gaze didn't meet hers. As if he was running through the events and sensations of the night and day again.

"I've always wanted a tattoo, but I was too chicken to get one because I'm a bit of a baby about things like needles and pain." And things like making the first move, or telling a man she wanted him or kissing him as if she didn't want to let go.

Take the plunge.

She took a deep breath to steady her nerves. With shaking hands—she was definitely not under the influence of anything now—Hayden stared for a moment into his brown eyes, willing herself to calm down. "I would have wanted you last night, and ordinarily I would have just…let it pass. Oh, I'd tell myself if it's meant to be it would happen, but that's just a very familiar excuse. You told me you don't do one-night stands, either, so I'm thinking I must have done a few other things last night, and I'd really like to know what those were."

Tony leaned back against the cushion of the booth

seat, his gaze thoughtful and probing. "So what would you do if you had no fear of the consequences or possessed any self-restraint?"

"Clearly you," she teased, and he choked back a laugh.

Her smile faded after a moment, though. "But honestly, Tony, I think it's more than that. Like I dropped the self-protection bubble and tapped into my primal instincts."

His fingers stilled her worried movements on the spoon, and he caressed the back of her hand. "Things you've blocked yourself from trying?" he asked.

She nodded. "Things convention and society says we should never, ever do."

"Something experience tells us we're not allowed to want," he added, his voice low.

"Last night I would have had no fear, and I would have wanted to feel *everything*." She would have wanted to feel his muscles tighten and grow taut under her fingertips. Indulge in the rough texture of his tongue as he laved her nipple. Relish the sweet friction of him sliding, hot and hard, inside her.

"Whatever you're imagining, Hayden, you've got to stop. You're killing me over here."

How must she look right now? Mouth wet and slightly parted. Skin flushed and heated because the blood inside her veins was pounding through her in excitement. Oh, yeah, he must have been able to read her like a book. The *good* parts of the book. Maybe fanning the back of her neck would help. Could she do that discreetly?

Instead her finger grazed the chain around her neck.

His eyes followed her movements as she traced the edge of the necklace and tugged out the key pendent that had settled in the V between her breasts. *Focus.* She was missing something here.

Hayden fingered the pendant, running the pad of her thumb over the sharp cuts of the key and cool plastic casing at the top. "Why would I wear this as a necklace? It's ugly. This is important—I know it. If it were just a key, I'd put it on my car key chain. Evidence notwithstanding, I'm very careful with my keys."

"I'm very careful with my car, so yeah, I understand."

She tapped the plastic with her nail. "It looks like there was a number etched on this, but it's worn off over time."

"That's a locker key, Hayden."

She smiled in excitement. "You're right! It's another clue."

Tony nodded. "Whatever we locked up, we wanted to protect. But where can you find keyed lockers anymore?"

"I can't think of one. Not even the airport or the train stations provide them anymore."

Tony grabbed one of the paper takeout menus and bummed a pencil off their waitress as she passed by. He began to draw a makeshift map with one large X for the cabin, an E for the casino and a line all the way to Dallas. "According to the map Mike gave me, there's not much between the Endeavor and Dallas but ranches and truck stops."

"You're saying the club and whatever this key fits must be in Dallas."

"If not, I'm out of ideas. At least practical ones."

Because she had all kinds of thoughts about implementing impractical ideas. Tony starred in all of them, mostly naked. Mostly? Who was she kidding? Completely naked.

"So last night we were up for anything."

"Probably the crazier the venue the better," she agreed.

Tony jotted *crazy place* on the menu.

"Maybe places where a little PDA is frowned upon." That little interlude they shared in the dressing room proved she'd apparently nursed a fantasy for nearly getting caught.

He wrote down *forbidden* next.

"Definitely things we've never tried before."

New adventure joined the list.

"I'll just stow away our menu of misdeeds." He folded the paper and then angled his hips to slide it into his back pocket.

"Menu of misdeeds, I like the sound of that."

He tossed his paper napkin onto his plate. "You ready?"

She nodded and stood, and Tony left some cash for the bill.

"I know Dallas is my town, but if you keep driving, I'll stay on the lookout for anything shiny along the road." After all, most of what they'd done appeared to have been *her* wish fulfillment. Hmmm. What did Tony fantasize about?

"Sounds like a plan."

The sides of the highway thickened with businesses and neighborhoods and hotels as they approached Dallas, and another lane joined the highway to accommodate the added traffic.

There'd been plenty of signs advertising dance clubs and sports bars but nothing really unique. Nothing that would have blurted out *Turn off the highway now—here is where you must go.*

But something did catch her eye. "Check it out," she said, pointing outside his window. "Ten o'clock."

"What? Do you see a club candidate? Is it behind the mall?"

She shook her head. "No, it is the mall."

Skepticism flickered in his eyes as he glanced at her sideways. "So your lack of judgment or moderation took us to the mall last night?"

"No, but my common sense and reason takes us there today. I'm sure they have a computer store there. We can log in and use one of those locate-my-phone apps. Might lead us somewhere."

"I sure reeled myself in a smart one last night." He changed lanes and aimed for the off-ramp. "Didn't realize people still went to the mall."

"Yes, Mr. California Excitement. This is Texas—we go to the mall here. Giant enclosed ones with carefully controlled climates, too. Let's pop over to one of those kiosks by the food court—we can buy a burner phone."

"Did you say burner phone?"

She began to giggle. "I guess I did. I like to watch

those clandestine spy shows on TV. I think the kiosk is called OnTheGoPhones. Does that work for you?"

He draped an arm around the back of her seat. "It all works for me."

"YOU WEREN'T KIDDING. This mall's kind of happening," Tony told her as they maneuvered around clumps of people standing in front of store windows and generally being way too slow.

"Why is it that everyone on the planet is in no hurry at the exact moment you want to get someplace fast?" she asked, but they soon found the mall directory. "The computer store is on the second floor, one spoke over."

They hiked up the escalator and reached the second floor at a record-setting pace. Only to stop at the large line in front of the store. "Oh, no. I forgot people were camping out here tonight to get the new phone on Monday."

A college-aged kid with a clipboard and friendly smile approached them. "If you take your spot here, we can't guarantee there will be any stock left on Monday. Your best bet is to order online."

Hayden leaned over and spotted dozens of people in the store, playing around on computers and music players. "What about if we just want to try out your products?"

He stepped aside. "That's free. Check out the new video editing software. It rocks."

"Oh, yeah?" Tony asked.

"Come on, Mr. Movie, we can play around with that later."

Hayden and Tony fled the crowd standing in line and joined the crowd milling around the store. Hip but catchy music played over the high-end sound system above their heads while they waited until a free computer opened up. After two failed attempts at remembering her password, a progress bar flashed on the screen. She crossed her fingers. "Here's hoping I have some battery life left."

A beautiful blue dot sprouted on the high-resolution wide-screen monitor, then a map appeared. "Yes!" she shouted. "If I were the kind of person who high-fived, you'd be so fived right now."

Tony shrugged. "I can think of other things we can do to celebrate. Still involving your hands."

"I'm going to ask you to share those with me later." Two could play the flirting game.

Hayden zoomed in and a little animated signpost appeared. Tony copied down the address and directions on the menu of misdeeds.

"Click on the signpost and see if there's a picture corresponding with the address. We could get a name of the business." But when she moused over that option, the picture was all blurred. "Must be a privacy thing."

"Which brings up all kinds of questions about what exactly this place could be." Her thoughts flew to the naughtiest ideas: sex club, burlesque theatre, adult toy shop—places where the patrons frowned on digital surveillance.

"And there's no phone number, either. This keeps getting more and more interesting."

"Guess we don't need the burner phone," she said and

logged out. Then she stepped aside so Tony could log into his account. Of course he remembered his password on the first try, but unlike her, no blue dot appeared.

"Phone must be dead. It gets a lot of use, so if I don't keep it charged, the battery goes down quickly. It's basically my portable office, and I can use it to get great video in places where it's hard to drag in a ton of equipment. I also use it to edit on the fly. I've got over eight hours' worth of video on the modern-day cowboy project on that phone. Not sure what I'd rather lose, my car or my phone."

"Maybe it's beside mine, it's just dead," she said trying to reassure him.

"Then let's go find them," he said.

They got back into the car and headed for the co-ordinates of her phone, but she still kept her eye out for a place that would have appealed to no-inhibitions Hayden. Luckily the early evening fall sky still provided plenty of light for her to keep searching out the window. But her shoulders slumped as they drove closer to her phone with still no club that appeared even mildly intriguing.

"Even if I find this place, maybe we should still go pick up my phone first. It's possible the club is not off the highway, but closer to where I left my phone. Heck, the club could be *where* I left my phone."

"True, but same as at the casino, I don't think a phone would be turned into lost and found. Too easy to pawn or get crushed under dancing feet."

Then she spotted it. "Oh, my God, Tony."

"Save that for later."

She tapped her finger against the window. "Look at that billboard. It's a place where you can actually swing from the chandeliers."

"You think that's our club?"

Excitement pounded through her. "Oh, yeah. I *know* that's our club."

"Where do we go first? Club or address?" he asked.

"How far away are the two?"

"Five minutes."

"Club." Because curiosity trumped common sense.

ONLY A FEW cars dotted the parking lot of Lavish, most likely staff vehicles, but Hayden suspected that by nightfall, there'd not be a free spot in sight and a line outside the door and around the building to get in.

"I've heard people on campus talk about this place, but now I understand why it's so popular," she said, pointing to the large placards on the building advertising the endless entertainment available inside. After you paid the cover charge, of course. Lavish seemed to cater to the most outrageous kinds of fun, and hanging from a chandelier was just one small example. They boasted one room full of foam, and another of snow, and of course, one room filled with a few mechanical bulls because they were in Texas. "My friends say the club has several different floors, each playing a different kind of music, from hip-hop to electronic funk. I think they even have a rooftop terrace for dancing when it's warm."

The front door was unlocked, probably as a convenience to the staff. They walked through a long, dark, draped hallway that distorted sight and sound and heightened the senses. Had she walked this hallway last night with Tony? Or had she met this sexy stranger here?

The hallway opened into a large room. Several brightly lit bars spanned the walls, along with inviting VIP booths, but the large dance floor dominated the space. She imagined the lights at their feet pulsing to the rocking beat of the music, but right now only a lazy test pattern lit the floor. The house lights were up and a waitress rushed past them, only to stop and glance their way. "You here about a job?"

Hayden shook her head.

"Then we don't open until eight."

"Actually, we're trying to find… That is, I think we were here last night, and…" She took a deep breath and tried again. "Can you swing from a chandelier here?"

The waitress squinted. "Oh, hey, I remember you now. Yeah, you two were wild about the idea of taking the swing. You had one of the private rooms upstairs. Number eight, I believe." And she pointed to a wraparound staircase, and moved on, too busy with setup to care about them anymore.

Signs inviting them to Ride It and Make the Thrill lined the stairwell. "They must get their suggestive advertising from the same company as the Endeavor." Tony chuckled.

"Well, sex sells."

The second floor had ten different rooms for private parties but also opened up to an elaborate balcony that overlooked the dance floor below. And there, secured to the railing, waited three swings. One was the prom-ised chandelier. The second was a gilded cage. The third was a bed with silky black sheets big enough for two.

"I bet we tried all three," Tony said, standing so close to her his breath tickled the hair at her temple. She shiv-ered at the intimacy.

She'd bet she'd kissed him on that bed, for once feel-ing sexy and daring because she'd finally dropped the self-protection and tapped into primal instinct. Stopped blocking what she'd wanted to try and what convention and society told her she should never, ever do. Did she have the guts to do it again? Completely clearheaded?

Something experience tells us we're not allowed to want.

Last night, had she been the experience Tony wasn't allowed to want?

"Let's check out room number eight," he suggested. She nodded, not trusting herself to speak. More than anything she wanted to be alone with him. To touch him.

Make the Thrill…oh, yeah.

He pushed the door open and shoved it closed be-hind them. Heavy drapes lined the walls in here, too, masking the outside noises and leaving only the sound of their breathing. Padded silken chairs were set up in intimate pairs in the corners and nooks of the room. A balcony took up the fourth wall so VIP guests could look out over the dance floor if they didn't yet need the privacy of the corners.

She crossed to the balcony. A DJ must have arrived to test the sound system, because a low rocking beat began to pump below them. The house lights lowered and the strobes began to pulse and flash with the music and her hips began to sway to the beat.

She felt Tony's incredible heat against her back. "Last night I would have rented all of these ten rooms if it meant I could have been alone with you. Wouldn't have cared about losing eight hours of video."

Her eyes drifted shut for a moment from the powerful effect his admission had on her body. She felt light and heavy. Her mind cleared and fogged. She turned to face him, the rapid rise and fall of her breasts a finger distance from the breadth of his chest.

His eyes grew black with desire and need. "It was all I could do to stay on my side of the booth at the diner."

"You were a mile away."

"All day has been one long buildup. Agonizing foreplay that has never ended," he admitted.

She began to sway to the music, her hips matching the beat of the music thumping below them.

"You've tortured me, all damn day, keeping me wondering when you were going to try to jog my memory again with a kiss."

She reached for his hand and drew his finger to her lips. She darted her tongue out for a quick taste then sucked his index finger into her mouth. His eyes closed for a moment as he groaned. "Whenever you use this finger, I want you to think about being inside me."

His gaze dipped to her lips. "You've got a mouth that…"

"That what?" She wanted to know. *Had* to know.

"Makes me want to do this." Then he hauled her

against the solidness of his body as his lips brushed hers. Once. Twice. His tongue slid along the seam of her lips, then stole inside her mouth, tangling with hers. His hands explored up and down her sides, cupped her ass and demanded a response.

This was old-school ravishment like the kind in her granny's historical romance novels. Only she wasn't an unwilling ingenue. Or unknowing. She sank her fingers into the hair at the back of his neck and pulled him closer, kissing him with all the ramped-up and tamped-down need that had been stored inside her since she'd woken up beside him tangled between the sheets in bed.

Or when he'd cupped her breasts and teased her nipples in the dressing room.

Or when he just stood beside her. Breathing.

If carnal temptation had a flavor, Tony must taste exactly like that. Erotic, sensual and heady. His hands circled her waist and drew her against him tightly. "Here," he whispered against her lips.

"Here?" she managed to ask after a long moment.

"Here, alone in the dark, is where I finally would have stopped fighting."

"Why here?" Her throat constricted and her stomach fluttered.

"Because I would have smelled your hair, heard you talk, felt that sexy body of yours all night." He laughed, self-deprecating and oh-so delicious. "Of course I sold my car." He cupped her face between his hands, his thumbs gently caressing her cheeks. "Because you, Hayden, *you* I want like nothing else I've ever wanted in my life."

Her body began to tremble and her nipples tightened almost painfully against the soft material of her cami. "I want you, too."

The DJ changed the music and a low thumping bass began to pound through the club. Red, blue and yellow lights pulsed along with the music, alternately filling the private room with brightness and casting them in darkness. Every few moments, the glow would gift her with a clear view of Tony—the tight angles of his face, the strain around his beautiful brown eyes—then the beams would shift again and he'd be hidden in the dim.

Tony pushed her deeper into the corner of the room. Into the shadows and against the wall. She met his mouth this time, opening for his kiss. Pleasure and excitement rolled through her. She lifted her leg against his and hooked her foot behind his knee, drawing his hips against hers.

The hardness of his cock brushed between her legs, sending a spark of naked thrills through her. She thrust against him and he groaned. She rubbed harder and gripped his ass and he groaned more, the sound of his erotic reaction inflaming her. "Mmmmm, Tony. You fit between my legs perfectly."

His breath rushed from his chest in a heavy exhale. "Hayden, you can't say things like that to me."

She thrilled at the roughness that spiked his warning. As if he was in exquisite agony. Good. That's exactly how he made her feel. Wanting and needy, and yet sexy and desirable. She swallowed and bit back a grin, excited to poke the bear a bit. "It's true, though. I want you, here, with nothing between us." She ground against him to prove her point, sealing her lips against his.

His rock-hard penis grew with every push of her hips into his.

With a tormented growl, Tony gripped her by the shoulders and spun her away from him, propelling her against the covered softness of the wall. The fabric cooled her forehead, which was tinged with perspiration. Her skin felt overheated and her clothes too tight.

He draped his chest against her back while his hands circled around her hips. She reached above her head, her hands drawing his head down. His lips found their mark along her sensitized neck. And oh, did his tongue find the sweet spot below her chin.

The tight knitted sweater rode up her stomach as the warmth of his fingers traced patterns on her exposed skin.

"This is what I wanted in that dressing room today," he told her.

"Me, too." And so much more. Hayden rotated her hips in time to the music until she found the hard ridge of his cock. Then she teased and tormented him some more. He jutted against the curve of her ass, and her knees almost buckled. If last night had been half this amazing she'd have been in trouble.

She performed a little shimmy, as if she was the stripper and he was the pole. Tony groaned against her neck, his breath teasing her skin. She swayed again. And again.

His hands cupped her breasts, molding and shaping them.

"Mmm, that feels so good. You make me feel so good." Her words sounded little more than a slurred moan.

"It's about to get better," he whispered against her ear.

His left hand continued to cup and shape her breast, holding her against him. Not a problem—she had no plan to leave. But his right hand—that questing right hand dipped lower. His fingers trailed oh-so slowly along her rib cage. The muscles of her stomach coiled when he slid past her belly button and sank under the waistband of her jeans. He gave her a light, teasing caress.

Her knees did give then, and he hauled her tighter against his chest. "Easy," he ordered, his voice sounding pleased by her charged reaction.

Hayden's mouth dried in anticipation of his next touch and the air in her lungs felt heavy.

But his hand didn't move.

"Tony?" Her voice was a groan of utter frustration laced with intense expectation. She wanted more. Needed more.

"Tell me you want me. *This*." He stroked her clit with the lightest of touches.

She managed to nod, a frantic movement of her head. Hayden leaned into him, nearly mindless, craving and so, *so* achy.

"Tell me what to do," he whispered, and she squeezed her eyes tight.

She licked her dry lips. "Touch me. Make me come."

His fingers found her clit again, but still he only gave her a light-as-silk stroke. Her muscles clenched as aggravation and disappointment warred within her. *Oh yeah?*

Two can play like that. She bucked against him, and his cock surged hard against her backside. "More," she ordered on a moan. She added a "please," just in case.

His soft chuckle vibrated through his chest and into her back, and damn if it didn't make her hotter. Then he stroked her clit fully and she moaned.

"Oh, yes, Hayden. Just like that. You have no idea what it does to me to hear that I'm giving you pleasure. That I'm giving you what you need."

"Don't stop," she urged.

Tony toyed with her. Teasing then stroking the sensitive bud between her legs until all she could feel, breathe and hear was Tony. She lived for the next touch of his fingers. Her heart beat with the rhythm of his fingers. Then his hand moved lower and he delved inside her moist heat. Prickles of sensation pummeled her, and she held on to his neck with what little strength she had left.

"You're so wet. How could I have taken it?"

"Taken what?"

"Not being able to rip off your panties and bury myself inside you," he told her, his voice guttural with need. Then he increased the speed and pressure of his strokes.

With her eyes squeezed tight Hayden leaned into his hand; the only sense she cared about right now was touch. A feverish bliss spread from her core to every tensed muscle and jazzed nerve ending she possessed. Her legs stiffened and Hayden hissed in a breath as she toppled over the edge of sensation, climaxing in wave after delicious wave.

Tony gently spun her around in his arms, and she

settled her cheek against the soft cotton of his button-down shirt. His heartbeat raced beneath her ear, and she managed a weak smile, knowing her pleasure at his carnal attentions had made his body react.

"That was without a doubt the most thrilling thing I've ever done in public," he whispered, his voice tight with unspent desire. Even the gentle slide of his breath against her ear elicited a tidal wave of shivers.

There should have been a moment of acute awkwardness in a situation like this. After all, the man had made her fly apart shoved up against the wall in a club while people on the floor below were setting up for the evening.

But Hayden's whole body felt sated and relaxed and too good for her to worry about what to say or how to act with the man who had driven her to this satisfied state with the caress of his fingers.

"I could listen to the sound of your moans every day until the moment I died."

She smiled and hugged him tight.

He snapped his finger. "I am a filmmaker after all. I could record you and listen to them anytime I wanted."

She reached for the hem of her top and gave it a few fluffs so it wouldn't resemble something that had been smashed against a wall. "Yeah, sure. Maybe make it your ringtone, even."

Even in the dark, she couldn't miss his narrowed eyes.

"Kidding. No," she told him flatly.

"Hello?" a voice called from outside the door.

6

"DAMMIT," SHE MUTTERED, frantically trying to smooth her hair.

"It's probably the manager. The waitress must have told him about us. I bet he just realized two people came up here and haven't gone back down yet."

Hayden might not feel awkward with Tony, but she'd be all kinds of uncomfortable if a stranger found out about her intimate encounter up here. Maybe being caught wasn't as enjoyable a fantasy as she'd suspected. "You think there's a back way out of this place? Maybe we can sneak out." She grabbed his hand. "C'mon."

But he was like a boulder that refused to move. "Hey, it's all right. So they found us making out up here. No big deal."

She'd forgotten that Tony wasn't exactly a stranger to getting caught breaking a few rules. "We did a lot more than make out." She had the tingling aftershocks to prove it. "Texas may be big, but it's uncanny how we seem to run into people we don't necessarily want to see. He's going to know someone I know, and then everyone will know. I've worked too hard, sacrificed too much to lose it now, and what just happened in there dances way past the indiscreet line. Behavior like that makes employers wonder whether I can make good judgment calls."

Tony ran his fingers through his hair and straightened his shirt. "Don't worry, you look great. He won't suspect a thing," he whispered.

Her back straightened at the rush of shivers his soft words evoked. "He will if you keep whispering at me like that."

The doorknob turned and a young guy with fashionable beard stubble, gelled hair and a loosened-for-effect tie popped in and flipped on the light switch beside the door. "There you are. Tanya said you two were up here. Did you find what you were looking for?"

"Yes," she stammered, blinking against the harshness of the light after being shrouded in darkness for so long.

"Almost," Tony responded a second behind her.

She bit the inside of her lip to keep from smiling. There'd be no almost for him the next time they were alone. She'd make sure of it.

"Then I guess you'll be on your way then," the manager said, opening the exit door wider.

So polite, and yet he was delivering a clear message: Get Out.

"You wouldn't remember us from last night, would you?" she asked. Of course they hadn't been throwing around Benjamins then or buying a car to paint like a ladybug, but they could have done some other crazy thing here that the club's staff wouldn't forget anytime soon.

Except the manager shook his head. "My night off, but the bouncer was here. He would have seen everyone who came through our front door," he said as he jerked his head toward the stairwell, clearly ready to get them out of his club. Not as polite.

They dutifully followed the manager down the staircase, across the flashing dance floor and back through the draped hallway. A big, beefy guy who had probably played offensive line in high school and college was chugging what appeared to be a protein shake while watching the Cowboys play on a small screen over the front door. The TV was probably a security monitor during business hours.

"These are the people Tanya was telling us about. As they were *on their way out*, they wanted to ask if you recognized them from last night." Then he glanced at them. "I'll leave you to it," and he returned to the club.

The bouncer angled his head from left to right as he stood behind his stand. "Oh, yeah, I remember you."

Her pulse quickened. *A clue, a clue, a clue!* It was almost too much not to dance around and high-five. What did football players do? Give a smack to the rump? No, spike the ball.

"You didn't want to take off your wristbands and put on ours."

And just like that, her excitement was doused. "But we did put your wristbands on. I've seen a picture." This could be the wrong club after all, but everything pointed to Lavish. "What kind of wristbands did we have on when we came in?

"Like those plastic, can't-take-off kind you're given at the hospital when you're admitted with a concussion or an MRI or something."

"Did we mention why we were at the hospital?" Tony asked.

"You think one of us got hurt last night?" Hayden asked to Tony. "Maybe we met at the emergency room." That might be why the tattoo hadn't hurt yet. Perhaps some long-lasting pain relief medication. Nothing on her felt sore, but then how could she really tell?

"That would be a story," Tony replied.

The bouncer only shrugged.

Tony returned his attention to the burly man. "But we eventually took the bands off, right?"

"I had to cut them off, but yes."

"Do you know if we took them with us or, uh…" she let her words hang. What a ridiculous conversation.

"I tossed them in the trash."

This conversation was about to get even more ridiculous. "Where would that trash be now? In a Dumpster out back?"

The bouncer squatted and looked under his desk. "You're in luck. The janitor hasn't pulled it yet."

Hayden sprang around and joined him behind the desk. "Hey," the bouncer bellowed.

"Really? I'm scaring you? You're like two and a half of me."

"My place." He made a wide circling motion encompassing the area behind the desk. "Your place."

Then he made the same wide circling motion where Tony still stood.

She suppressed a heavy sigh. "You're right. That was rude of me. I'm just pretty desperate to find those bands."

He crossed his thick arms. Those muscles couldn't be real. Men didn't bulk up that big unless they'd taken something. "How can you be? You didn't even know about the hospital bracelets three minutes ago."

"The information that's on them is what we're desperate for. We've been trying to piece together what we did last night."

His lip lifted in a smile. "Oh, so you don't remember. Don't doubt it. They must have let you out of the hospital way too early because you were flying high on something."

The manager laughed at that, announcing his return. The waitress from earlier, Tanya, right behind him.

Hayden and Tony passed a quick glance. Another clue. So nothing was slipped into their drink here. They had come here already under the influence of whatever.

"Could you do us a solid and let us look through the trash?" she asked.

"No."

"Seriously? You didn't even pretend to think about it."

"Yeah, I'm just messing with you. Be my guest." The bouncer stepped aside so she could go behind the desk, this time with an invitation. A small office-size trash can filled with receipts and who-knows-what else waited for her on the floor.

She squatted beside it then glanced up at the manager. "You serve food here, right?"

He nodded.

"Then I'm sure you have some latex gloves in the kitchen? Maybe another trash bag?" she asked with a forced smile.

"I'll be right back," Tanya offered.

"So who's winning the game?" Tony asked the bouncer while they waited. Was that small talk or was he interested? Perhaps something to file away for Project Getting To Know The Man You Plan To Romp On Later. Growing up in Texas, it was difficult not to like football, so she stared at the little screen right along with them.

"Not us. Damn running backs."

Tanya hurried to them with the gloves and another trash bag.

Hayden thought about asking if Tony would like trash duty, but then, he'd made her explode in his arms just a few moments ago. Plus she'd done her fair share of dirty work the past couple of years trying to pay for school; so unfortunately, trash detail rested firmly in her wheelhouse. She snapped the gloves in place and crouched down next to the trash can. With a flick of her wrists and a whoosh she opened the extra trash bag, and then sank her hands into the trash.

"Gross." The bouncer laughed.

Hayden glanced up to see Tanya and the manager staring down at her, laughing along with the bouncer.

"Have none of you ever watched someone dig around in trash before?" she asked, which just made them all laugh harder. Okay, she must appear pretty ridiculous, and she smiled at Tony for a moment then she refocused on the task in front of her. A new person wearing a janitorial uniform joined them, too. Whew! They'd cut it close.

With techniques an archeologist on a dig in Greece's ancient ruins would have been impressed by, Hayden lifted a ballpoint pen, dozens of cash register receipts and scrunched-up napkins from the garbage and stuffed them into the new trash bag.

There! Close to the bottom rested two plastic hospital bands.

"Found them." *Yeah, take that, trash!* Cue the guitar riffs and anthemic chorus because she felt a power song coming on.

The first band had a black ink blot, most likely from a ballpoint pen explosion, that obscured the name of the hospital and its address. Useless. Hayden tamped down a groan of frustration. She grabbed the second band, and although there was ink smeared across the hospital's name on this one, too, the address was clear.

She lifted the band in triumph for all to see. "Same address as where my phone is located." Hayden stuffed the rest of the trash inside the bag, carefully slid off her gloves and tied the trash bag shut.

"You wouldn't mind taking that out to the Dumpster out back for me, would you?" the janitor asked.

She and Tony stared at him, but he only shrugged. "What? You've already done most of it."

Hayden had to laugh. "Sure, but you'd really make my day if you told me a phone has been turned in." Tony's might not be with hers. There was still a chance it could be here.

But everyone shook their heads at her hopeful question. "A phone would be long gone by now," the manager said.

She stood and pumped into her palm a glob of hand sanitizer from the bottle left for patrons at the bouncer desk. Gloves or no gloves, she still wanted to wash her hands, and she was pretty sure they'd worn out their welcome here at Lavish, so there'd be no using the restroom.

The Dumpster stood in the same parking lot as their car. "I can't believe you still took that out for them," Tony said as he opened the passenger door for her a moment later.

"It was the least I could do. They did give us our biggest pointer so far."

"It was a pleasure to watch you work," he told her, then kissed the tip of her nose before she got in the car.

Her nerves began to shoot off again as they neared the address on their bands, but it wasn't a hospital or clinic that waited for them—it was an inconspicuous medical office. Affixed to the wall rested a sign stating PharmaTest with its hours of operation. Closed today. And tomorrow, but Tony tried the handle anyway. Locked up tight.

She felt like stamping her foot. "Oh, we were sooooo close."

"But at least we have some answers. We weren't drugged, at least not maliciously. PharmaTest sounds like one of those volunteer drug testing facilities."

"That makes sense. I used to volunteer a lot for those trials because until recently I didn't have health insurance and these drug testers will sometimes give you a full checkup along with some cash. Usually I get sorted into the placebo group. Not this time—full side effects. It's been a while since I volunteered for a trial, but I still can't believe this wasn't one of the first things I thought of."

"Well, whatever they gave us messed with our memories, so a side effect could be our short-term reasoning abilities."

"Did you just make that phrase up?" she teased.

He chuckled. "Maybe. It makes sense that I came here, too. I've been tossing around the idea of a documentary on big pharma and the testing cycle and trials behind our meds. Thursday night I must have stopped in here to conduct some field research and ended up volunteering."

"If I hadn't needed a bit of extra cash to buy my graduation gown, or if you'd decided to stop at some other research facility, we might never have met."

But Tony was somewhere else. Distracted.

"What color is your car?"

"Yellow. Why, do you see it?" She scanned the lot behind her until she spotted her beat-up hand-me-down sedan in the lot across the street from Pharma-Test. "Tony, that's it! Have you ever laid your eyes on anything uglier or more beautiful than that?"

"I'd say Ladybug, but…"

"Ladybug was a work of art," she defended.

But her current car? Hayden had always had a love-hate relationship with it. Of course she didn't look down on reliable transportation, but with its distinctive yellow color, her friends loved to joke that she should hire herself out as a taxi to earn extra cash. She grabbed his hand. "C'mon, maybe we locked our phones inside."

The parking lot was close enough to the offices of PharmaTest that it would register as the nearest address on the mapping application.

She dug into the pocket of her jeans as they ran toward her car, tugging out her keys. She opened the driver's side and then reached across the seat to unlock Tony's door. He eased in beside her. "You check the glove box while I look in the console," she suggested.

"Nothing."

"Nothing here, either," she said, letting the lid drop into place. "The phones must be inside the testing office."

They had their answers now. At least most of them. What she didn't know was what happened next.

"So Monday…?" she began slowly. Trying to prompt him.

"Monday," he agreed.

Here's the point where she should put the *romping* part of Project Getting To Know The Man You Plan To Romp On Later into effect, but she was suddenly shy. She wasn't sure where to look or where to put her hands.

And dammit if Anthony Garcia wasn't acting the gentleman again and giving her space and time to decide what she wanted to do next. This sexy man beside her had reached for her or tried to kiss her every time they were alone, and now they were damn close in the tiny confines of her car. Yet the man kept his hands to himself.

And stop cursing him, she told herself, because he was actually being very respectful and she should damn well appreciate that and not be frustrated.

Only she didn't want him to be a gentleman.

Well, there was only one way to get what she wanted; she had to lay her cards on the table. She licked her dry lips and glanced his way. "Tony."

His gaze bored into hers.

"I may not remember how we got together last night, but I know why. You are, without a doubt, the most incredible guy I've ever met. I'm glad whatever happened to us last night happened. Maybe it let me put my guard down so this could happen."

She stroked the side of his face, the prickly stubble sending thrills through her. "This would be a lot easier if you kissed me," she admitted.

"Ask me to kiss you," he urged.

Instead she took the initiative, as she had with their first kiss to jog their memories. She drew his mouth to hers and kissed him. Long and slow and savoring. Heaven. Booyah—she could do old-school ravishment, too. His mouth parted beneath hers and Hayden pressed herself to him as close as the center console would allow. The heat and scent of him wrapped around her, honing her need of him to a fine point.

"I don't want to stop," he muttered.

"Then don't." But he'd already pulled away from her. Rubbed his chin. She'd witnessed that move enough times to know that was his go-to thinking action. Then he gazed at her, his eyes half-lidded, the pupils molten.

"Not like this, Hayden. I want a bed and you and…"

"And?" she prompted.

"You and a bed and forty-eight hours. Hell, seventy-two."

"No food?"

"Always the practical one."

"Barring the evidence of this weekend, yes." Then her smile faded. "Are you staying in Dallas? A hotel?"

Once she would have thought offering herself up to a man for a weekend of nothing but sex seemed like a tough play to pull, but in reality, it was deliciously easy. Her bed, Tony and seventy-two hours sounded absolutely perfect. Except…

What happened after seventy-two hours? What if she wanted more? *If?* Hell, she *knew* she'd want more. It would take a long time to work a guy like Tony Garcia out of her system.

"I had a hotel, but with no key, no wallet and no ID, I don't think they're going to let me in because I ask nicely."

"Well, you look pretty, too," she teased.

"Still, I doubt it's going to happen. Guess I have to call the DMV on Monday, too."

Hayden lifted her car keys and jingled them. "Well, I happen to have keys. And a bed. And time."

He sucked in a heavy breath. "You're sure?"

Gallantry like that could make a woman fall in love. "Follow me in your car?"

"I'll be right behind you," he told her as he reached for the door handle.

"Mmmmm, has possibilities."

She watched in her rearview mirror as he strode away from her. In about an hour she planned to be ripping those jeans from him, and then locking her ankles behind that back.

But they'd only managed to drive a block when she abruptly pulled over and parked the car. He was outside her door before she even had a chance to unbuckle her seat belt.

"What's wrong? Are you okay?" Tension laced his voice.

"Sorry, I didn't mean to worry you. Look." She pointed to a long, aluminum building with neon lights along the roof.

"A roller rink? You want to go skating?" he asked, his voice unsure.

Hayden reached for the chain around her neck and lifted the locker key. "The skating rink is the only place I can think of around here that still has lockers. And look at the sign advertising what they feature on Thursday night."

"Adult skate. Wow. Hayden, you may have actually got me inside to skate. Let's go," he said taking her hand, his fingers lacing through hers. They ran together to the entrance.

Heavily synthesized disco music greeted them. Mirrored balls and strobes flashed on the traditional hardwood floor of the rink. Lights and music seemed to have been the theme of last night. And sex.

"How much?" Tony asked the attendant.

"Open skate is six bucks. You can rent in-line or regular skates inside for more."

Hayden waved the locker key in front of him. "Actually we just want to check something inside and return this key to the locker we used last night."

The attendant nodded. "Six bucks."

Tony chuckled, then reached for the cash in his pocket.

"No," a loud voice yelled.

All three of them whipped around to see who was shouting and why. A very angry man wearing the black-and-white-striped shirt of a referee rolled toward them. He pointed toward the exit. "No. I told you last night you were no longer welcome here."

Holy cow, what had they done? This was a new re-action. No one had ever been angry with them before. Not Darcy at the Endeavor. Or Mike and Betty. Not even Jeff.

"We're not welcome at a skating rink?"

The ref rolled his eyes. "Of course you don't remember. High as kites, the two of you. I hate adult night. I'd rather deal with a bunch of middle schoolers."

"Actually, we were under the influence of medication," she began to explain.

"Under the influence, for sure. You were deliberately going the wrong way against the crowd. Shooting the duck. Shouting, 'Carpe Nullam.' What kind of grown people get caught making out? At a roller rink?"

Apparently she still harbored that make-out-at-the-rink-with-a-boy fantasy from when she was thirteen. Which she'd obviously indulged in here. And at Lavish.

And the cabin. And probably all the way from Texas to Oklahoma.

Hayden flashed him the locker key. "Just tell me if this is one of yours or not."

"You're still having trouble with the 'not welcome' part, aren't you?"

Tony flashed him some green. "What about my friend Alexander Hamilton. Is he welcome here?"

The ref snatched the money from Tony's hand. "The lockers are by the concession stand. You can check them… On. Your. Way. Out."

Hayden slunk off toward the lockers like a chastened middle schooler, but that embarrassment vanished as the three rows of lockers awaiting them came into view. They raced along the bank of lockers, each one with a key in the lock until they came to the beautiful last row—and there it was. A locker with no key. The angels could sing now. Rainbows could form and unicorns roam free.

Hayden tugged the chain up and over her head and aimed the key at the lock. It fit. It turned. "Whoo hooo."

Tony twisted the handle and opened the door.

"My phone!"

"My purse! No DMV trip for me."

"That's a cause for celebration in itself."

"No kidding."

Tony's phone case also held his ID, a credit card and a hotel keycard. "Looks like no DMV trip for you, either."

Tony's head swooped down and her lips met his and it—

"No. Stop it right there. I am done with you two. Out."

They ran from the skating rink hand in hand, laughing and truly carefree for the first time since this morning. "I'm staying at The Briarwood. Which is closer? Your apartment or my hotel?" he asked when they reached her car. "I can't keep my hands off you another minute."

"Your hotel. Driving across Dallas to my apartment could take an hour with traffic. Your hotel is definitely closer."

His hands spanned her hips and he drew her closer to him. The hard ridge of his cock made her shiver. "I don't want to wait."

"Hotel it is," she agreed with a smile.

He reached into his phone case and plucked out his hotel keycard. "Take this in case we get separated. I'll get another at the front desk."

"Tony you don't have to—"

"This thing between us, it's unexpected and so damn exciting. We've been nonstop since this morning, charged on nothing but adrenaline and adventure. I want to kick my own ass for saying this, but I want you to take a moment. Maybe go back to your apartment. Use picking up your toothbrush as an excuse."

She wanted to argue with him. She just wanted him. Right now.

He cupped her cheek, the rough pad of his thumb a soft caress. "I could deal with a lot of things, but not your regret. Never yours. I don't ever want you to look back at this weekend and wish for something different."

She nodded and silently took the keycard from his hand and slipped it inside her purse. Strange, she was usually the cautious and careful one, whereas he was the risk-taking filmmaker. But from what she had pieced together of his childhood, he had also been raised by a woman filled with regret. A woman who had blamed him for how her life turned out.

Hayden didn't need the extra time, but Anthony Garcia needed her to take it. So she'd give him that.

Besides, he was right about the toothbrush. She could also use a bra in case they decided to escape the room for a meal. But that was it. The rest of the weekend she planned to be naked with this amazing man.

"I'll be there," she promised.

He dropped a quick kiss on her lips, tender and filled with promise. "I'll be waiting. And Hayden…"

"Yes?"

"If you come, I'll want every one of those hours in bed you promised."

7

BY THE TIME she arrived at Tony's hotel over two hours had passed. Traffic had refused to cooperate, traveling first slow, then crawling to a standstill on the highway. Then maybe she shouldn't have opted for the quick shower in her apartment. She'd also taken the chance to pack a few more things than a bra, her phone charger and a toothbrush. But she hadn't seen the harm in the extra couple of minutes. Until it was two hours later.

Hayden tossed her overnight bag onto the passenger side of her car as the sun slipped over the horizon. She should text or call to let him know she was running late. No, not text—call. Rudeness was worth a phone call. Then she realized she didn't have Tony's number—or her phone. So much for Project Getting To Know The Man You Plan To Romp On Later.

When she got to the hotel, the helpful attendant at the front desk connected her to his room, but Tony didn't answer. By the time she strode into the hotel elevator

Hayden felt terrible. He'd probably assumed she'd had doubts and bailed out of their date.

The elevator dinged, announcing she'd arrived on his floor. She found his room, but hesitated before sliding in the keycard he'd given her. As late as she was, maybe she should knock.

Or maybe he was in bed, naked, and she'd ruin that pleasant setup by making him come to the door.

In the end she opted to key in as planned. She shoved the keycard in the swiper and the green light flashed. The door opened up to a mini suite. A large window presented her with a gorgeous view of the Dallas nighttime skyline. A couch and chair situated in front of a large TV made up the seating area. Nearby was a small breakfast bar with a coffeemaker, microwave and refrigerator in the corner. A large ergonomic workstation took up almost the entire wall, and it was partially covered with camera and editing equipment. An open door led to a very empty bedroom. Where was he?

The bathroom door snickered open and Tony emerged, framed by billowing steam, a white hotel towel draped low around his hips.

She swallowed, because her memory hadn't done justice to the rock hardness of his stomach. It was almost unfair how gorgeous the man was, especially when you tacked on smart, funny and charming.

A sexy, slow smile eased across his face when he saw her standing there. "Was beginning to think you'd changed your mind."

She flashed him a faux pout. "Too bad you're done

with your shower. Hotel shower sex just happens to be one of my fantasies."

He stalked to her. "Later," he growled against her throat.

The handle of her overnight case slipped from Hayden's fingers as he hauled her up against him in one powerful move. "Hayden, you are wearing too many clothes."

He kissed her then, hot and hard and possessive. With one sensual flick of his tongue, she opened her mouth to him and moaned. Finally giving in to what she'd been waiting for. What they'd both been waiting for. She gripped the sides of his head to keep his lips against hers as he cupped her breasts. Her nipples tightened, growing needy and hard beneath his palms.

The towel slipped and dropped to the carpeted floor and Tony stood against her, lean and naked. *Finally.* She couldn't get enough of touching him. She ran her fingers along the corded muscles of his back, loving the tethered male strength she felt beneath her fingertips. Then she sought the hardened cheeks of his ass, stroking his skin and relishing his reaction as his muscles tightened and clenched from her slightest of touches.

His fingers lifted to caress the skin exposed by her shirt. "That V-neck you wore today has done nothing but drive me crazy since the casino," he moaned against the swell of her breasts. "Then other times it was that chain you wore nestled between your breasts. Agony."

In one quick movement he grabbed her hips, lifted and balanced her on the edge of the worktable. He reached for the hem of her shirt and peeled it up her body, then over her head.

"Too bad you wasted time putting on that bra," he teased. He found the clasp in seconds and tossed it aside. He sucked in a breath as he stared at her breasts. Her nipples pebbled beneath the hunger of his gaze.

"I can't wait to taste you." He lowered his head to her body. The feel of his lips on her overheated skin exhilarated her. Her head fell to the side, and Hayden arched her back to give him more of her. She was being greedy and didn't care. He laved one of her nipples as his fingers found the other, plucking and teasing.

"I wanted you so bad at that diner. There I was with this funny and sexy woman, and I couldn't do a thing about it."

"Do something about it now," she urged.

His hand dropped between her thighs. Never had there ever been a more frustrating barrier than denim. His fingers teased and stroked her through the fabric and she lifted her hips toward him, offering herself up for more, more, more.

"I remember thinking that if you hopped up on the table and reclined, I could stand between your thighs. I could watch your breasts bounce with each of my thrusts."

"That would certainly draw a lot of attention." She aimed for a teasing tone, but her words hung between them like warm molasses.

Tony drove against her then. She felt the power of his hardened cock, and her temptation to tease instantly died. Need, hot and desperate, flooded her. As if he sensed the change in her, he thrust against her again.

"I think this desk is just about the same height as the table," he said. "I'm going to do you here."

Her legs began to tremble at his admission. "Yes. Here," she urged, her voice filled with longing. All thoughts of gentle lovemaking and a bed faded away. She wanted hard, pounding sex, as if they were two people who couldn't wait to walk three steps away from the door to begin.

His fingers worked the metal button of her jeans, and he kissed the skin he exposed. Then he tugged down the zipper at a slow and agonizing pace, but when the task was done, he rewarded her with another kiss just above her bikini line. Followed by a lick. The trembles began again.

"Where will you kiss when my jeans are off?" she asked.

"Let's find out." He reached for the waistband and began to tug. She helped and soon her jeans lay in a crumpled heap on the carpet. Tony stroked her through the silk of her panties that separated her clit from his touch. "You're so wet. You really know how to bring a guy to his knees, don't you, Hayden."

The agonized roughness of his voice *would have* brought her to her knees if she weren't splayed out before him on her back on a table in his hotel room.

He worked her through her panties—light grazing touches, then full forceful strokes. Already her inner muscles were contracting. "Tony, I'm not sure how much of this I can take."

"Don't worry. I plan to make you come all over this room."

She felt an orgasm rising, but she willed it down, wrapping her legs around his hips and locking her feet behind him. His cock brushed her exactly where she needed it. "Oh, yes, this table is exactly the right height."

"You don't play fair," he told her as he surged against her. "Let me make you feel good like this." As he had in the club? Her greedy body begged her to say yes.

She rubbed against the head of him, the pleasure almost sending her over the edge. "I want you to make me feel good with you inside me."

With a groan he reached for something behind her. When she heard the sounds of ripping foil she knew she'd won. He tore at the lacy scrap that blocked his entrance until it gave way. He flung it behind him and his fingers grazed her clit. She bucked against him and grabbed his shoulder. "Now." It rang out more like an ordered plea.

He shifted his hand away and gripped his cock between his fingers. Then he probed her opening with the tip of his penis. "Are you ready?" he asked.

"Are you kidding?" She'd been ready since before she'd keyed into his hotel room.

He answered her with a low chuckle, then slid into her until he was fully seated. She sucked in a breath as she adjusted to the hard length of him. He was big, and it had been a while, but she was ready. His thumb found the throbbing pulse of her clit and gave her a gentle swipe. Within the circle of her legs he pulled away from her then thrust back in to the hilt.

"You good, Hayden?" he asked, his voice strained.

She could only frantically nod, her hips lifting, seeking more of him. He stroked the sensitive bud again as his other hand reached for her breasts, teasing her nipples while he thrust in and out over and over.

Hayden angled her hips to meet his thrusts, and then her orgasm hit her, powerful and fierce and her moan echoed around them loud and primal. A moment later, she realized Tony was still hard within her. She balanced on her elbows to look at him. "You didn't…"

"Oh, there's a lot more I want to do," he informed her. Then he scooped her up in his strong arms and marched toward the couch. "You drove me crazy tonight in the club, your ass cradling my cock from behind."

He set her on her feet and turned her away from him, facing the couch. She nestled against the heat of his chest, his cock hard against her cheeks.

"Bend over the side," he told her.

She leaned down, her fingers sinking into the soft cushion of the couch, her backside high in the air.

"Perfect—perfect angle, perfect view," he groaned. He fit his hips to the curve of her backside, and slid into her from behind. She sucked in a breath from the pleasure of this new position. He reached between her legs and stroked with each of his pounding thrusts, heightening the sensation.

Her legs trembled again, but she had the help of the couch to prop her up. He surged harder within her, his fingers stroking and rubbing until she grew nearly mindless with the pleasure.

"Come, Hayden. I want to hear that sexy groan again."

As if on command a shiver of delight took over her body, and she groaned until he took his fingers away from between her legs.

He gently pulled away from her, and she sagged against the couch. She sucked in breath and willed her legs to stand because she had some work to do. Tony still hadn't come. And that was about to change.

He began to lead her to the wall. His next fantasy? Not this time, buddy. Right now *her* fantasy was to hear his groans sounding in the hotel room. Right. Now.

He tugged again, but she shook her head. Her fingers wrapped around his shoulders and she gently shoved him down onto the couch. She straddled him before he could sit up. "Now I'm going to make you come," she told him, and his muscles lost the will to strain against her.

She tongued the curve of his ear. Sucked his earlobe into her mouth. "This is what I'm going to do to your cock later."

His big beautiful body shuddered. "You can do it now."

She couldn't stop the smile on her face. "True, but you already have the condom on. Don't want to waste it. I like to be environmental like that."

He thrust his hips against her, his cock grazing against her sensitized clit. "This is environmental?" he asked.

"It's definitely elemental," she replied, and without

notice she lifted her hips and sank down the length of him until he had no more to give.

"You just killed me, Hayden."

"Then you're really going to miss out when I do this." And she raised herself along his length then descended.

"Yes. Just like that, babe," he told her, his voice tight with need. His hand sought her breast and he brought her nipple into his mouth. He laved and sucked until all thought fled her mind and it was filled only with delectable sensation.

She rode him with no restraint until every muscle tightened and the pleasure grew too much. "Now, Tony. Come now."

He thrust up and she tumbled over the edge, her climax more intense than all the others before it. He roared as he came, his cock pulsing inside her.

Spent and sated, she dropped her forehead to his shoulder and licked at a spot below his ear. "That was incredible," she murmured, and then she could no longer keep her eyes open.

How LONG HE dozed on the damned uncomfortable couch in his hotel room, Tony couldn't say, but the soft weight of Hayden in his arms felt right. How could that be? He'd known her for less than twenty-four hours, correct that, he *remembered* her for less than twenty-four hours, but he'd never wanted a woman the way he desired Hayden.

The fantasy of her in no way competed with the reality of her. Mind. Blown.

They'd never made it back to the bed, and by her

steady, even breaths, they wouldn't be stretching out across that big king-size mattress anytime soon. Hell, he didn't really want to move anyway. He liked her just as she was, worn out from their hot and heavy sex and wrapped across him. So instead he tucked her head into the crook of his neck.

Hayden pressed her lips to the column of his throat and kissed him in her sleep.

If the sex had blown his mind, that almost dropped him to his knees.

Twenty-four hours and already he had feelings for her. That was a prospect that loomed heavily. But one he'd face later. In two weeks he'd be gone. Back to California and half a country away from Texas.

Sex fatigue made his arms and legs heavy and he fought his drooping eyelids. Tony reached for the spare blanket the maid had draped on the back of the couch. They might still be sweating from their bout around the hotel room, but the air would chill her skin soon enough. He rotated his shoulders so he could lie lengthways on the couch, drawing the sleeping woman tighter against him. He fell asleep with the sweet scent of her filling his senses.

THE DELICIOUS AROMA of coffee teased her nose. Hayden stretched and smiled because last night she'd had the most amazing night with a man, and she actually remembered it. Dependable orgasms. Oh, yeah, baby. She'd been right about him all along.

Okay, she could stay on this really uncomfortable couch and gloat about how good Tony had made her feel last night or she could find that dang coffee. Coffee always wins.

The blanket he'd tucked over her shoulders dropped to the carpet as she stood. She stooped to pick it up and wrapped it around herself, catching his scent. Tony stood behind the breakfast bar, brewing her a cup. Apparently he'd been playing his own version of Project Getting To Know The Woman You Plan To Romp On Later. Coffee first thing in the morning? He made it really tough for her to think of him as someone who'd be out of her life soon.

But their lives were definitely headed in different directions. He was a California filmmaker and she hoped to be getting a final offer from Hastings Engineering, headquartered squarely in Texas. *Remember that.*

He'd tugged on a pair of jeans, but hadn't bothered to button or zip them. All the better. She padded barefoot toward him. He turned as she approached and flashed her a smile that blasted heat all the way down to her toes. Tony handed her the coffee mug.

"You remembered."

"I've witnessed the carnage of an uncaffeinated Hayden," he teased.

"It's true. I can't even be mad you called me out on it." She wrapped her hands around the warm mug and breathed in the roasted nutty scent, part of her morning coffee ritual.

"I stopped by the drugstore next door and picked it up before you got here."

She tapped her finger on the ceramic. "That must

have been why you didn't answer your room phone. I called yesterday to tell you I was running a bit late."

He leaned across the bar and kissed the tip of her nose. "That call would have saved me a ton of anxiety after the first hour of waiting."

"I don't actually have your number, and I bet you don't have mine."

Tony advanced to the ergonomic workstation where his phone was charging. He unlocked the screen, pressed the contacts button and handed her his cell. "Plug it in," he invited.

"I dunno, this is a big step," she said, but couldn't manage to keep a smile from spreading across her face.

"I'll risk it." Then he watched as she followed the dating ritual and punched her number in. "I ordered some room service. It should be here in about thirty minutes."

The man really needed to stop being so perfect. "I have an idea for what we can do while we're waiting."

His eyes darkened again and he glanced toward the open door of the bedroom with the unused bed. "Not sure we'll have time. I want to savor you this morning. That's why I ordered the provisions. Have to keep my strength up."

A new batch of shivers chased down her spine and pooled between her legs. *Savoring.* She liked the idea of that. "Tempting, and something I will definitely be taking you up on later, but I really want to watch one of your films."

Tony straightened and shook his head. "You don't need to do that."

"I want to," she reassured him.

He tugged her hands into his. "Hayden, I like you. I can't think of anything I'd rather do than spend these next two weeks I have in Texas with you, but—"

"Wait, what? You want to spend the next two weeks with me?"

He laughed, but the sound was a bit hollow. "I don't know how two weeks will be enough, but yes, I want to spend them with you. But I don't want you to feel obligated to watch one of my films or think I expect that of you."

Had none of the women in his past wanted to share this aspect of his life? And why wouldn't he expect the woman he shared his bed with to be interested in what he did outside of bed?

Hayden wasn't sure whether to make her response teasing or truthful. Her instinct was to go for the joke. They both liked to cover emotional situations with humor, but she suspected Tony hadn't been on the receiving end of much heartfelt truth.

"This is part of you, Tony. I'm interested in what you're passionate about. You told me a film camera turned your life around. I want to experience it all."

Hayden watched his Adam's apple bob as he swallowed. Hard. Without a word he spun on his heel and walked toward his computer, then stopped and returned to her. His fingers curled under her chin and he dropped a searing kiss on her lips.

Hayden sensed what his reaction meant. He found it hard to deal with his emotional response to her request so he'd cloaked it with a physical one.

Then as quickly as he'd come toward her, he crossed toward the workstation, powered up his computer and placed it on the coffee table. She joined him on the couch, snuggling up to his side and drawing the blanket over both of them. "Let's watch your first documentary. The one that got you nominated."

"*Lost Causes*. It's about the street kids in Los Angeles. Some find it…tough to watch," he warned.

"Then that's the one I want."

He moused over the various media on his computer until *Lost Causes* appeared on her screen. From the first few moments she was riveted, and even when their food arrived she wouldn't stop watching.

By the time Tony had these kids' stories on film, they were already beaten. Broken. Her throat tightened with emotion. He hadn't just filmed these kids like an objective and uninvolved reporter; he'd lived with them. Knew them and struggled right beside them as they battled. She imagined he hadn't grown up much different from the boys he'd recorded. Lost cause. Was that how he'd thought of himself? How he still thought of himself?

But then about halfway through the movie, something changed. Each one of the kids interviewed was given a chance. For one it was a bus ticket across the country to Raleigh to live with a grandparent. Another was gifted with an easel and paints and a spot in the same center where Tony had lived. All opportunities. A shot, and a glimpse of the possibility of living a different kind of life. The last ten minutes of the film updated their stories each year until the present.

She brushed at the tears in the corners of her eyes as the credits rolled.

"Told you it was rough."

"Rough, yes, but Tony, you did something amazing with your subjects." She gripped his hands in hers, squeezing as she spoke. "Most of those kids just needed a shot. Like you with the transitional center and finding that camera. You made that happen for them. Sure, not all those guys rose to the challenge, but there's so much hope and optimism and anticipation in your documentary, I'm…moved. Overwhelmed. Inspired. By you."

"Hayden, I… I—" and then his lips were on hers in the sweetest of kisses. Poignant and tender. He nipped at her lips, then slid inside her mouth to trace lazy circles against her tongue.

His hands caressed her everywhere. No part of her lacked his gentle ministrations. "You remember that savoring promise from earlier?" he asked, his voice little more than a ragged whisper.

She nodded.

He stood and extended his hand toward her. Things between them had just become real. She'd had that same thought the day before, but now what stirred between them was deeper. More personal.

She clasped his hand and they walked side by side into the bedroom where that king-size bed beckoned.

And there Anthony Garcia savored her.

8

LATER THAT MORNING after showering and rubbing each other clean, they finally tackled the breakfast muffins and bagels he'd ordered from room service. As they ate, Tony showed her some of his film equipment in the sitting area.

"Subjects like the cowboys don't mind the more sophisticated cameras, which is good because the wide-open shots look great with the better gear. With the sunsets and the flatness of the terrain, this will be my most visually appealing documentary. But when I film the kids, it's usually just the camera on my phone. Makes it more personal, and this generation is all about the phone. It's so much a part of their lives already, they barely notice it. Keeps it real."

Hayden traced the outline of his phone case with her fingernail. "Have you ever filmed, you know...?"

"What?" he asked.

"Oh, c'mon."

He shrugged, his expression innocent. Well, as innocent as a sexy beast like Anthony Garcia could manage.

She tried not to roll her eyes at him for forcing her to say it. "Have you ever filmed a woman strip for you? Make love to you?"

"Are you offering? You *are* trying to kill me." He quickly raised both palms. "I mean, don't get me wrong, I'm fine with your technique."

"Oh, I plan to keep you very much alive for this showing. How much money do we have left of our winnings? If I'm going to do this right, I want to buy some sexy lingerie." She tore off a corner of her muffin and popped it into her mouth.

"If we had no money at all, there'd still be cash for that," he assured her. "In fact, take my credit card, *cariño*."

Hayden giggled. "The leftover cash should do just fine."

Tony kissed her long and hard, his hands growing possessive. "*Te adoro*," he whispered against her neck, his voice deep and rumbly.

"You've never spoken Spanish to me before." She'd have to look up that phrase, but she suspected it was something to do with adoration. Yeah, Hayden adored what he did to her body, as well.

"My *tio*, Hector, made sure I knew Spanish. He was in the army and wasn't around much after I turned four, but he's retired now. He was my guest at the Academy Awards, but still razzed me about how awful my accent is."

"I think it's sexy."

"I'll tell him that the next time he gripes at me. Now you were saying something about really trashy lingerie?"

"I don't think I used the word *trashy*."

"My mistake, but since you brought it up, you can never go wrong with really trashy. In fact, I'll come with you," he offered.

But she shook her head. "This is my surprise. And the operative word I'll be using for this lingerie will be *classy*. But I promise you won't be disappointed."

"How could a man be disappointed when his woman is offering sexy?"

His woman? She escaped to the elevator because that earlier kiss may have messed with her senses but his words messed with her mind. *Te adoro.*

Hayden had barely noticed the expansive hotel entrance last night, but large indoor water fountains graced the lobby. The furniture was simple and elegant, but most importantly, the concierge was helpful. She directed Hayden to a nearby lingerie boutique only a block away. Hayden wouldn't even have to take her car.

The display windows on her walk invited her to shop. Watches and jewelry and coats and the most gorgeous black boots she'd ever seen filled her vision. Maybe one day. She'd be getting a steady paycheck once she started her job. When she made the last student loan payment, those black boots—or something similar—would be hers.

The lingerie boutique did not have a window display, just a simple and graceful sign over the door announcing Bliss. She pushed open the champagne-colored fabric-lined door. A tiny bell pleasantly tinkled her arrival. Hayden immediately understood why the concierge had suggested Bliss. This wasn't just shopping—it was an experience.

The lightly perfumed air invited the sensual, and everything from the lilting music to the subtle lighting evoked only the pleasurable and pleasing.

The most beautiful woman Hayden had ever seen slunk over from behind a counter. From her curly hair to her dark eyes, she exuded confidence. She was so comfortable in her own skin and who she was, Hayden felt awkward in her jeans and T-shirt.

Wow, would she ever be half so poised and self-assured? Hayden wondered. So at ease with her own desire? Her own sensuality? She loved her gran dearly, and Hayden knew she'd only wanted to give her young granddaughter the best, but the sex education she'd provided was designed more for someone born before the sexual revolution. Her grandmother had taught her to be cautious and to stay focused on her schoolwork. Which had been great for her education, disastrous for her love life.

Granny, I love you, but I'm going a different way.

"Oh, I know what you need," the saleslady told Hayden with a graceful smile.

"Wait, but I haven't even said what I wan…" But the woman had already glided to a row of intricately carved wooden drawers against the wall. She opened the drawer, revealing bras of the most delicate pastel pink and yellow, to the rich hues of fine emeralds and rubies. The woman lifted a stunning bra for Hayden to drool over. No, this was a brassiere. Both lacy and silky, Hayden would feel incredible in that striking lingerie. Dangerous. Perfect.

"The corset-fit cups give you the support you need while allowing you to indulge your daring side. The ruched-ribbon straps caress your skin and the lacy over-lay satisfies your feminine power. The iced mint color will make your eyes pop."

"Not that he'd be looking at my eyes."

"Oh, you'd be surprised. A smart man will be able to see in a woman's gaze if he's pleasing her."

Tony must be a freaking genius then.

"You really did know what I needed. *I* didn't even know I needed this, uh…" Hayden searched for a name tag.

The saleswoman smiled. "Keely. Now tell me what you came in for," she said.

Here's the part where Hayden should be mortified. With Hayden's work and study schedule, she'd been more interested in climbing under the sheets to sleep than discussing what happened between them. But yeah, she was in a place called Bliss about to talk crotch-less panties with a stranger, so she simply announced it out loud. "I want something sexy that I can take off for a man."

Keely paused for a moment, nodding but also giv-ing Hayden that scrutinizing side-to-side look. She was being sized up, for sure. "I have just the thing. But first, remember you are taking your undergarments off for you. Because *you* want to feel the slide of silk along your skin. Because *you* take care of your body and don't want to hide the innate sensuality women are always being told to be ashamed of. The fact that he's enjoying the show…that's a bonus. For the both of you."

This is for me. Hayden's mouth twisted. Hmm, not totally buying into it.

"How do you feel when you look at yourself in the mirror? Naked?" Keely asked.

"Uh, I feel the overwhelming urge to spin around," she joked.

But no smile graced the woman's lips.

Hayden crossed her arms against her chest. "I dunno… I sort of…you know."

Now Keely lifted a brow. "Dunno, sort of?"

"I sound like an insecure thirteen-year-old girl, don't I?" Hayden admitted, her laugh awkward and devoid of humor.

"That girl doesn't always leave us."

"I find that hard to believe about you." The woman basically glided as she walked, oozed sexiness and probably never had to worry about rejection a day in her life.

"Young girls and women have a lot in common. They want to please the people around them. Women take into their heart too much of what they hear. And while caring about others is a woman's strength, it's also a weakness, because she stops caring about herself. That ends when you buy that first piece of lingerie that's just for you."

Like a mint brassiere with ruched straps. So impractical for an engineer, and so just what she needed.

Keely made a wide sweeping gesture. "Turn around

and face this mirror. Now tell me how my lingerie will make you feel."

"Sexy. Desirable."

"Go on, dig deeper. Sexy and desirable is how you want to appear. How do you want to *feel*?"

"Dangerous."

"Good."

Hayden's eyes grew fierce. "As if I'm putting the man I'm with on notice to bring his A game."

"When I showed you the bra earlier, did you once think about how he'd like it, or only how much you'd enjoy wearing it?"

Her eyes widened. "Only me."

"See? No thirteen-year-old girl. We tell ourselves that men are attracted to large breasts and flat stomachs and perfect thighs, but the man you want to be with, he's drawn to you by the confidence you exude. That comes from pleasing yourself." Keely lifted a finger. "Now, you can keep your man in mind, of course, there's nothing wrong with that. It's not like you wear pink because you discover he hates the color. Yes, his tastes are important, but please yourself first. You said you want something to take off in front of a man?"

"It sort of popped out of my mouth in the moment. I had a thought, and I went with it." Because it made her feel bold. Provocative.

Keely nodded. "Your instincts are good. Now let's give you the tools. What colors strike you most?"

"I'm drawn to bold colors. Deep purples and reds."

"I have just the thing."

An hour and a half later, Hayden hesitated in front

of Tony's door. She was about to make a video of herself in a compromising position—just the kind of thing she'd been afraid she'd done Thursday night. The kind of thing that could jeopardize all she'd worked for.

But Hayden knew something now that she hadn't known yesterday—Tony was honorable. An old-fashioned word learned from Gran, but still it applied. He would never allow such a video to get out. And for herself, the one thing she'd learned in the past twenty-four hours was that her own fear and inhibitions had been keeping her from a whole host of pleasurable experiences. And she wasn't going to deny herself anymore.

Hayden slid the keycard inside the lock and the mechanism released with a click.

Tony stood as she entered, shirtless with his jeans riding low on his hips. Could there be a sexier man than this one? How was she supposed to play out her striptease fantasy when all she wanted to do was yank his jeans down?

His lips curved in a smile while his eyes darkened with relief.

"Afraid I wasn't coming back?"

His grin turned rueful. "The idea had crossed my mind. Hayden, you don't have to strip while I film you. It would be amazing, but don't do it if you—"

"Your camera ready?" she interrupted, tossing her purse onto the coffee table.

His nostrils flared as he sucked in air. Hard. The sound loud and telling. Her heartrate kicked up and the blood pounded through her veins. The heavy ridge of him grew behind the zipper of his jeans.

You're doing this for you.

But the fact that her man had obviously been anticipating it so much was more than just a bonus. It was a pleasure that made her feel dizzy, and so very wanted.

Wait. Her man?

No, she was just confused from the sex haze. She and Tony were enjoying one another. There was something empowering about dressing for a man, knowing you had his full attention—when he wouldn't, no scratch that, couldn't look away. But as the saleswoman had told her, it was even more empowering to dress for her own enjoyment and pleasure.

She lifted her bag from the boutique. "I'll be right back." Then she slinked—or at least she tried—into the bedroom. She closed the door behind her, the bag clutched to her chest. The bed was made. Tony or maid service?

The Do Not Disturb Sign had still been hanging from the door when she'd returned, and their dirty breakfast dishes had been stacked but not cleared. No, Tony must have made the bed. Now that she thought about it, the bed at the cabin had been straightened, too—once she'd no longer required the sheet as covering. It was the little details that made a woman truly know a man.

Her granny had always been a stickler for bed making, a habit Hayden had gleefully dropped in college.

She slumped to the edge of the mattress. Somehow knowing Tony had straightened the bed here and at the cabin softened her heart. Surely it was not something he'd learned as a kid in the chaos that had surrounded him. Must have been the transitional center, where he'd learned the discipline and order that had saved his life.

Hayden smoothed a wrinkle out of the comforter. She could learn to make a bed again, maybe like it even, but first...

She unbuttoned her jeans and shimmied them down her legs to her ankles where she kicked them aside. Then she reached for the thin hem of her top and tugged it up and over her head, creating a pile as she added it to her jeans. After unclasping her bra and slipping out of her panties she stood naked. She caught sight of her amplified image in the floor-to-ceiling mirror. She sucked in a breath. As always whenever Hayden accidentally saw herself in the mirror, her go-to reaction was to shift her gaze away as quickly as possible. But no longer. Sure, there were flaws there, but that was no longer her focus. Tony adored her body. Her thighs didn't have to be perfect and her stomach didn't have to be sculpted.

From now on she would dress for herself. Well, when her first paycheck arrived.

She reached for the delicate black thong panties. Not cotton and definitely nothing elastic. Granny would be scandalized. *Good.*

Hayden caught the reflection of her smile in the mirror. She looked like a carefree woman ready to claim her pleasure.

After stepping into the panties, she tied the wisp of lace in place with delicate silk ties at her hips.

More black lace waited in her bag. For something

so frothy and light, it had cost a fortune. *This was for her.* Worth it.

Hayden allowed the expensive silk nightie to brush along her arms; the sensuality of the lace teased her skin, eliciting tiny tingles.

Black French lace and boning cupped her breasts, then sheer, bold purple fabric stroked the curves of her waist and floated at the top of her thighs. Hayden felt sexy and powerful and desirable and deserving. Everything Keely promised at Bliss. This wasn't just a bonus; she was about to walk up to the free-throw line and score in the double bonus. And now she was into basketball metaphors instead of poker ones.

Feeling confident, Hayden opened the door to find Tony fiddling with his phone and waiting for her on the couch where they'd made love and slept in each other's arms the night before.

"Tony," she whispered.

He looked up, and his eyes widened and his jaw lowered.

First free throw and nothing but net.

"I was right earlier. Dying from sex with you is really the best way to go."

"You know, at first I imagined drawing you into the bedroom. I'd slowly strip for you, and once I was completely naked I'd drag you onto the bed." Her fingers glided along the black lace strap holding her baby doll nightie in place. His gaze drifted to follow her movements for a moment, then met her eyes once more.

A smart man will be able to see in a woman's gaze if he's pleasing her. Yep, her guy was a genius.

"Next I'd straddle your hips, and then sink down the length of you slowly until you filled me perfectly."

Tony cleared his throat and stood, stalking toward her. "And now you actually have a better idea? Because that one sounds pretty damn amazing."

"Sit in the chair if you know what's good for you."

That perfect ass of his landed on the cushion so quickly a thrill of excitement raced along her spine.

That's right, Garcia.

She fled the protection of the bedroom door frame and followed him out to the sitting area of the suite. His hands shot out toward her as she neared him, but she shook her head.

"Not…yet."

A sheen of perspiration broke out across his forehead as she stood before him. Her nipples poked at the delicate fabric, hardening under his gaze and the anticipation of her touch. But not yet.

Hayden trailed her fingers up and down her legs, drawing the sheer purple fabric up, giving him a glimpse of the black satin of her thong panties and the tiny purple bow that rode just above her clit. She allowed the fabric to fall back into place. Hayden couldn't stop a small smile when he groaned.

"Aren't you supposed to be filming this?" she asked.

He swallowed and rubbed his chin. Two tells. This little striptease was doing a number on him, and she'd barely even started. "Hayden, you don't have to," he reassured her again.

"Camera," she reminded. "It will keep your hands busy. C'mon film guy, time's a wasting."

Heat fired in the dark depths of his eyes. Tony grabbed his smartphone from the coffee table, swiped the screen and punched in the code. He dropped into the chair, leaned toward her, his muscles taut. In anticipation? Oh, yeah, a ton of anticipation.

That's it—you settle in for a show.

"Now, where was I? Oh, yes, right about here." She smoothed her palms along her waist the way he liked to touch her. Exactly how he liked to grip and stroke her.

"You've been paying attention," he said in a strained voice.

"Oh, yes." She cupped her breasts, molding and lifting them until they grew heavy and achy. She teased her sensitive nipples through the lace, tweaking and plucking until her head rolled to the side in pleasure. With a final light pinch, she traced the edge of the lace at the swell of her breast. Goose bumps formed along the weaving path of her fingers.

His hands wrapped around the wooden armrests of the chair, as if it was the only barrier holding him back from reaching for her. His phone lay forgotten on the hardness of his thigh. She gasped as she spotted the hard ridge of his penis behind his jeans.

"You're not filming this."

Tony lifted his phone and peered at her through the screen. "I am now."

Hayden looped her index finger around one slim black bra strap and gave it a gentle tug. It slipped over her shoulder and down her bare arm. Then she performed the same ritual with the opposite strap. Tony breathed in deeply as the other strap fell, then exhaled heavily when only the black lacy cups held her baby doll nightie in place.

"Are you ready for more?" she asked.

Tony's fingers whitened around the edge of his phone and he nodded.

With one small shimmy of her shoulders, the lace fell and bared her breasts.

"*Cariño*, you are the most beautiful woman I've ever seen."

Cool air brushed her breasts and her nipples puckered.

"I want to kiss you. Your mouth… I dream about those lips." Tony stood and her heart beat in anticipation of his mouth on hers. But then Hayden remembered *she* was running this show and she wasn't ready for audience participation quite yet. Except, instead of reaching for her, he reached for the light switch to turn off the overhead light and flipped on the lamp by the desk. "The shadows play along your skin as you move."

"That a director's trick?"

He nodded. "Guess I'm into pain since I just made this harder on myself."

With a sensuous twist of her hips, the black and purple lace slid down her sides to tickle her thighs and pool at her ankles. She circled his chair as she stepped away from her nightie, giving Tony a view of her thong. Hayden worked her hips as she dragged a hand around his shoulders. His muscles bunched beneath her greedy fingertips.

He gifted her with a ragged groan and bit out something in Spanish she didn't understand. But she didn't need to understand because craving and desire were etched in every hard angle of his face and in the rigid control of his muscles. His naked want forced a carnal response from deep inside her, and her vagina clenched. She hadn't planned on this little striptease to be tortuous to her, too.

"Remember at the club when you had me shoved up against the wall?"

He glanced at her from behind his phone. "Uh-huh."

"You thrust your fingers down my pants and your cock was up against my ass. I wanted you then."

"I know. You came." The camera followed her movements as she orbited his chair.

She paused when she stood in front of him, and dropped her hands on either side of the chair, leaning on the armrests. She moved toward him, her lips close to his ear. Would he respond to her breath against his skin as much as she'd responded to him? "I wanted you to take me against the wall from behind. I didn't care if we were caught. I was mindless. You *made* me mindless."

His next breath was a shudder. "You can't say stuff like that if you want me to keep taping."

"Oh, babe, wait until you see what I have planned next," she told him. *Then* she'd wanted him against the wall. *Now* she wanted him in this chair. To rub her naked body against his as he sat below her watching. Filming her. Wanting her.

She lowered herself down to his lap, fitting the bulge of his cock between her legs. The sensation was exquisite. Hayden hooked her legs behind the back of the chair then leaned away, giving him a full view of her bared body. She ground into his cock.

Tony continued to film. "You don't know how much I want you."

She rocked up against him and he groaned. "I think I have an idea," she teased. She pushed herself upright again only to lower and raise herself against him, giving him a taste of what she wanted next. He lowered his head to her nipple, drawing the sensitive tip of her into his mouth and sucking. Spikes of sensation shot up her back and she moaned. She ground against him again until he was moaning, too.

"You're supposed to be filming," she reminded him once she caught her breath.

"Don't worry, I am," he told her against her skin.

Her eyes drifted shut from the pleasure of his mouth toying with her body. But she steeled herself. *Not yet.* She drew his mouth from her breast, unwrapped her legs from behind the chair and shimmied off his lap. She dropped her hands onto his knees, drawing his legs apart and bracing her weight on him. Hayden lowered her head and she wiggled her backside higher in the air, stopping only when her lips perched just inches away from the bulge of his hard cock.

"Is that what you have planned?"

"Later," she promised, and his eyes squeezed tight for a moment. Then she pushed away from him, and turned her back to Tony. As she spun in lazy circles before him, Hayden alternated between swinging large and tiny figure eight motions with her hips, rolling her hands along her skin, her fingers playing with the bows on her hips.

"In the club, I thought my legs would give out when you slid your fingers beneath my panties," she said over her shoulder. His gaze alternated between staring at her ass through the viewfinder and with his own eyes.

"You were so wet. I had to touch you. *Have* to." His voice was a pained thing, tight with aching need.

As he watched and filmed, Hayden slid her hand down her stomach and slipped her fingers beneath the black lace of her thong. Eyes half-lidded, she sucked in a breath and arched her back when she grazed the knot of her clit.

Hayden gazed at him through the camera. "I'm touching myself the way you did."

His eyes closed again, but then after a moment he zoomed in for a tighter shot of her erotic display.

She gave herself another rub, her body growing slick. "I'm thinking of you right now. Touching me here. Sliding inside me. Remember at the club when I sucked your finger in my mouth and told you to think of me whenever you used that finger? I'm imagining that finger doing such naughty things to me." The bulge beneath his jeans grew huge, and she licked her lips in taunting anticipation. She slid a finger inside her and closed her eyes on a moan of satisfaction. "I'm imagining that this is you," she whispered.

"Hayden." Tony's voice grew huskier, deeper.

"When you speak Spanish to me it makes me hotter. Wetter."

"Quiero un beso."

"More," she urged and tugged on the bow holding her thong together on her right side.

"Eres hermosa." That hint of an accent that flirted with her grew thicker and sexier.

"Mmmmm, nice." Hayden reached for the bow on her left side only to stop. "Not yet. I have more to do. To you."

"Hayden, I—"

She interrupted his words when she stood between his legs and turned, dropping into his lap. With a quick stretch, he balanced his phone on the side table, and then his hands moved everywhere on her body in frantic movements. Cupping her breasts. Dragging his palms down her rib cage and stomach. His fingers paused just a moment to tear away the remaining bow holding her thong in place, then found the wetness between her legs.

"Te necesito," he whispered against the back of her neck, and she shivered. "Lift your hips."

Ready and desperate for him, she lifted her hips and heard the sound of the zipper of his jeans drawing down. He tongued her ear, drawing the lobe between his teeth. "Torturess. You have me in pain." The rip of foil followed next, then the hot tip of his cock teased her, thick and throbbing.

Hayden raised her hips, then he was sliding inside her just as she'd imagined when dreaming up this fantasy. His hair-roughened thighs beneath her, she pushed against him. Never had she felt so good. So abandoned. So out of control.

He gripped her breasts to steady her, palming and plucking at her nipples until she wondered if she could come from just this stimulation alone. Tony rained kisses along her shoulder, nipping at the delicate skin of her back with his teeth, intensifying her pleasure. Then his fingers found her clit and she exploded in an exquisite haze. He cupped her intimately between her legs, drawing her tighter to him, and then he shuddered and pumped within her, calling out her name over and over again as he came.

She sagged against him. Spent. Staying in the chair until the air-conditioning cooled their skin.

"Up you get, *cariño*," he told her sometime later, and he gave her a playful swat to her thigh. "I want you in bed and nowhere else."

"Heaven," she breathed as she slipped between the sheets, and after a moment Tony joined her. He'd shucked his jeans and padded into the bedroom naked, gorgeous abs and all, clutching his phone in his hand. "Oh, we didn't get everything."

He made a scoffing sound. "Please, I am a professional."

"No, I distinctly remember you using both hands."

He eased in beside her on the bed, drawing her body flush against his. "I know how to set up a camera to take in a wide shot. See?" With a swipe of his finger the last few minutes of the video appeared on the screen. Their bodies shadowed by the lamplight, the sound of their breathing and thrusts echoed from the speaker.

Sweat broke out along the back of her neck as she watched the video, as this incredible man stroked her nipples until they hardened into points. Then she watched his hand dip between her legs, her reactions on the video subtly matching the muted reactions she was having now as she relived those moments. "Wow, that's actually pretty hot."

"There's a reason couples like to record themselves."

"Okay, so now delete it."

His brows drew together. "What?"

"Seriously, I've read too many articles of just this kind of thing coming back to haunt a person, no matter how many precautions she takes. So check the cloud or whatever, too."

"How am I going to relive this moment?" he asked.

"The old-fashioned way. You'll remember it," she teased.

He kissed the tip of her nose and clicked the delete button.

A screen popped up. *Are you sure you want to delete? Once lost, cannot be recovered.*

Hayden's laugh was half groan, half chuckle. "I hate these pop-ups. It's like our technology is doubting my decision, and then I start to second-guess myself."

Tony clicked the *Yes* button with his index finger before she could talk herself out of her original choice. With the sound of paper crumpling, her video was gone.

"Besides, I'll just give you something better to add to that memory," she promised.

"Starting when?"

"Now, if you're up to it."

Sometime later, they stretched out beneath the covers. Tony stroked her hair as she lay against his chest. His heartbeat pounded beneath her ear, strong and steady as he drifted to sleep.

Don't want this too much was her last warning to herself before her eyes closed and her body could no longer fight to stay awake.

9

ALTHOUGH PHARMATEST DIDN'T open until nine, Hayden could not fall back asleep on Monday morning. She'd woken up in the middle of the night, wrapped in Tony's arms. Exactly where she wanted to be. Which was the problem.

Because despite the great sex and the shared laughter and the adventure that bound them together, they'd only known each other a few short days. And she wanted more. So much more.

But of course it couldn't work. He lived in California and her life was here; she'd reminded herself of that at least six times a day so she wouldn't grow accustomed to him always being near.

Tony would be leaving Texas soon and then onto his next film—the one about drug testing. A spark of hope had fired up within her when he'd mentioned that Texas sported the second-highest rate of clinical drug trials in the United States, but that hope had burned out when he'd also dropped the factoid that California had the most. Why wouldn't he base his documentary in his own backyard? And there was no way she was leaving Texas after working so hard to secure a career here.

She eased out from under the warm, delicious weight of Tony's arm and padded to the bathroom, shutting the door quietly so she wouldn't wake him. A warm shower might relax her enough to fall asleep before the sun broke through the horizon. Otherwise she'd be exhausted when they met with the PharmaTest personnel, and she needed a clear head.

After turning the spigots to heat up the shower water, Hayden made herself busy setting aside a towel and making sure her shampoo and conditioner waited for her on the side of the tub. After another moment, she stepped beneath the spray, letting the water pound her body, easing the strain and tension from her muscles.

Hayden could fool herself and chalk up her anxiety to what would surely be a stressful interview with PharmaTest. Just how had they got out of the study area to traipse around Dallas clear up to Oklahoma? They deserved answers, and Hayden hated anything even remotely resembling confrontation. *Ah, yes, avoidance, my old friend.*

She squirted a dollop of shampoo into her hand and massaged it into her hair. Tony had washed her hair the last time she'd taken a shower. She'd been a soapy mess when he'd finished, nearly using half a bottle, but she'd remember the soft feel of his fingers massaging her scalp until she was old and gray and couldn't remember much of anything else.

So yes, while the discussion with PharmaTest loomed

daunting, the moments with Tony once the meeting concluded loomed even more threatening. Because then she and Tony would have their answers about the past, but only more questions about their future.

She stepped under the spray of the water and allowed it to take the shampoo away. After soaking her hair in conditioner, she then focused on lathering up her body. Her muscles were delightfully sex tender, her skin gently abraded from bouts against the wall, over a couch and from Tony's stubble.

Did she want a future with Tony?

Hell yes, was the answer. Her first answer. But then she had to think, did she *really* want a future with Tony? First take away how wonderful he was in bed because that would just cloud her judgment.

One, he was unselfish. She sighed. Good start, already getting somewhere. Two, the man always made sure she reached her pleasure first. And that time at the club, she was the only one who'd reached fulfillment. Wait a moment—she was supposed to be cutting out the sexual considerations because they scrambled her thinking.

Hayden turned the tap to a cooler temperature and rinsed the conditioner out of her hair. Shivering, she twisted the tap off and reached for the towel. Patting herself dry, she came up with the third great thing she knew about Tony—second if she discounted the sex—he was considerate. He took great pains to find out how she liked to be touched. Where. The man always delivered the perfect blend of pressure and friction when he stroked her cl—

Okay, hold up. She'd just veered back to the sex. But Tony *was* very considerate; she just had a difficult time separating his consideration in the bedroom from outside of it. That was normal, right?

What else must exist between successful couples? Comfort. Was she relaxed and at ease with him? He always made sure she was comfortable with the intensity of their lovemaking. Hell, he'd asked her twice if she was okay with filming her striptease when she was the one who'd suggested it.

She was doing it again. It was as if her reflections morphed into one of those dirty Insert Word games. Insert *in bed* after every thought with Tony.

He was interested in her ideas—in bed.

They shared clear communication—in bed.

Patient and kind—check and check—in bed.

And that was the problem—they didn't really know each other outside of bed. They'd got the order of things a little backward. Couples were supposed to learn whether they enjoyed being with one another first, then set the sheets on fire with the sexual chemistry. Hmm, maybe there was something she could learn from her gran's old-fashioned ideas about dating.

Outside of the sheets, he made her laugh. Ding ding ding! She'd finally thought of one trait that didn't involve sex, too. Even at her most worried moments in Oklahoma, Tony had been able to make her laugh. To relax and even enjoy the strange ride they'd been on together.

He wasn't weird about money. Woot—she was on a roll. Her last boyfriend had always insisted on going

Dutch, even though he'd already landed a very lucrative engineering job at a major oil-drilling firm in Fort Worth while she had still been struggling to make ends meet with temporary student jobs that paid crap. Still, her ex had insisted on going to expensive restaurants downtown and had scoffed when she offered to cook to avoid paying her pricy dining bills. After she ordered a glass of tap water and a side salad for the third time in a row on a date, he broke up with her, letting her down easy by informing her they weren't going in the same direction.

But Tony hadn't made a big deal about splitting the money from their casino winnings or keeping track of who'd spent what amount. It was almost as if they were already a team—a couple.

She closed her eyes and breathed deep, then faced what she did, indeed, really want: a shot at being a couple with Tony. After wrapping a towel around her head so she wouldn't get the pillow too wet, she flipped off the light and quietly opened the door.

Tony's phone lay on the bedside table because he'd set it to wake them up in the morning. Out of habit, she touched his phone to wake it up and double-check the alarm settings. As an engineer, Hayden relied on technology for everything, but for some strange reason she trusted a digital clock plugged into a wall more than a tetherless phone. Tony had given her his password so—

Hey, that was another thing they had going for them outside the sheets. Trust. The man had given her the code to his phone. That was like the key to a mandiary. The level of his faith in her made her smile, and yes, the alarm was still set for a few hours from now. She stifled a yawn. The shower and her decision about working toward a future with Tony allowed her mind to finally turn off so she could go to sleep. All the cool couples were doing long-distance these days.

She was trying to slide the phone to the off position but instead hit the photos icon. There, smiling back at her was a picture of her and Tony. A selfie from Thursday night. With the flashing lights and giant mirrored ball in the background, she knew they'd snapped this picture at the roller rink.

Hayden traced the outline of Tony's strong jaw with her fingertip. Sure would have been nice to have had this picture two days ago. Then maybe things would have worked out a little differently with Tony.

But would she really have wanted anything different? No.

With a smile, she swiped through the photos to see if they'd taken other shots. The next one showed another couple. Friends of Tony's? Okay, searching through his pictures had now officially morphed into snooping. She almost clicked out of his photo app when she realized the other couple were also at the roller rink. Hayden squinted and pinched her fingers on the screen to zoom in on various elements of the photo. Same wooden skating floor, and in the corner behind the smiling couple, lockers. Like the one where they'd stored Tony's phone and her purse. Exactly like the one.

Had she and Tony been at the rink with this couple, or was it just a random accident their image had been stored in his pictures? Had they been so loopy on what-

ever PharmaTest had doped them with that they'd made
friends with everyone in the rink? The manager said
they'd been beyond obnoxious.

Only one way to know for sure. She swiped to the
next pic. Now it showed Hayden and the mystery woman
making goofy faces, still at the skating rink. Hayden
scrolled though the photos quickly until she came to a
change in venue. A parking lot. *The* parking lot outside
of PharmaTest.

Why hadn't they looked at these photos before?
They'd been desperate to find their phones for just this
reason. Was it because once they were about 99 percent
sure they'd been given some kind of test drug, they no
longer needed an actual record, or was it because they
simply wanted this weekend together for themselves?
With not a single intrusion?

"Tony, wake up," she whispered, and rubbed his shoulder.

He groggily mumbled something in his sleep and
reached for her. His fingers curled around her upper
thigh and stroked. "You feel so good," he told her, his
voice indicating he was more asleep than awake.

A smile lifted her lips. Tired Tony was just as sexy
as fully conscious Tony. And car-adventure Tony. And
giving-orgasms-against-a-wall Tony. And waking-up-
deliciously-naked-in-a-cabin-in-the-middle-of-nowhere
Tony. Her blood was already heated in eagerness to explore just-woken-up-Tony.

Okay, sister, tamp it down. This was serious.

She gently shook his shoulder. "Tony, look at what
I found on your camera."

"I hope that means more lingerie."

She shook her head. "No, it's a photo."

"Mmm, sounds good. Come over here, *cariño*."

Her body curved toward him, ready to enjoy her some Tony and— Wait. Stop! "Tony, I think there was another couple with us at PharmaTest."

His eyes widened and a frown formed between his brows. "What?"

"I was checking the alarm on your phone when I accidentally triggered the photos to come up. And, well, look." She thrust the phone into his hands and he scrolled through his photos.

"That's definitely the outside of the PharmaTest building." He sat up and reclined against the headboard. The sheet slipped lower down his body, giving her a teasing taste of what she was missing out on at the moment.

"I began racing through all these scenarios in my mind. If we lost our memory of Thursday, maybe they did, too, but maybe they weren't so lucky. Remember how we managed to really irritate the manager at the skating rink? Honestly, it could have been so much worse than simply being asked to leave. They could be stranded or missing. Or they could be in custody."

He steadied her trembling hands with the warmth and strength of his. "Or they could be at home in their beds. They may have been given placebos or didn't have the same kind of reaction we did. PharmaTest opens in a few hours. We'll ask about this couple then."

"Let's hope PharmaTest kept better tabs on these two than they did us. I don't have a good feeling about this." Her stomach twisted.

He cupped her face and smoothed her bottom lip with his thumb. "We did just fine. Better than fine," he reassured her with a kiss to the tip of her nose. Then he returned his phone to her. "Here, search the internet on my cell. Comb through the local news sites for reports on couples exhibiting unusual behaviors and arrests. I'm going to take a shower."

She watched the masterpiece of his naked ass as he strode away from her and into the bathroom.

Understanding—another trait she admired in a man. She loved how Tony hadn't scoffed or blown off her concerns. And just to play along with her earlier game, he definitely understood her between the sheets.

Fifteen minutes later, he emerged from the shower, rubbing a towel through his short dark hair. Moisture beaded on his chest and shoulders and she fought the urge to lick those water droplets off with her tongue. But there were people to find. Maybe. And in a few short hours, after they had their final questions answered by the personnel at PharmaTest, she could indulge in her latest fantasy with Tony.

"Find anything?" he asked.

She shook her head. "No. Thank goodness, but I just have this feeling like I should be calling the police or something."

"If that's going to put your mind at ease, then do it. A nonemergency number should be listed on the Dallas PD website."

After explaining the situation to the person answering the telephone, she was connected to an officer a few moments later. "Missing Persons."

"Hi, uh, I think there may be one or even two people missing." Then a thought, probably a remembrance from some distant police procedural drama she'd watched on TV aeons ago, made her pause. "Oh, wait, aren't there rules and such about how long a person has to be missing before a report can be filed?"

"The DPD does not stipulate a precise amount of time. We ask citizens to use common sense before calling us," responded the officer, as if she'd spoken those words dozens of times and had them memorized.

Common sense—yeah, well, there was the sticking point.

"That's the thing—I'm not really sure if they are even missing."

"What are their names?"

Hayden clutched Tony's cell phone tight. Ugh, she was an idiot. "I don't know," she admitted.

"Let's try descriptions. Hair color."

Whew, a question she could answer. "She's blond and he's a brunette."

"Age?"

Hmm. About her age or so. "Ummm, I don't know."

"Ma'am, what do you know?"

"I believe we were in a drug study together. My… friend…and I lost our phones along with our memories, but then we located one of our cells at a locker in a roller rink and there were all these photos of another couple. The other couple is the one I'm afraid is missing, but I'm just not sure. Has anyone else reported four people missing on Thursday night? Because we were kind of missing, too."

"What was that you said about drugs?" the officer asked after a long pause.

Her body froze in place and her cheeks heated in complete mortification. "Um, actually, I really don't think there's a problem here. Thanks for your time, Officer. Sorry if I wasted it." And she ended the call.

Tony's lips twisted as if he was trying to hold back a laugh.

"That was a bust," she told him.

Then his shoulders began to shake.

"Yeah, ha, ha—I used your phone to make the call," she reminded him. "If anyone has caller ID it's the DPD."

"I'm sure the police have more to worry about than a crackpot who's reporting a few people who may or may not be missing. By hanging up, you just saved that officer a whole lot of paperwork."

Her shoulders slumped.

"Hey, hey, it's okay," he soothed, dragging her into his arms. "I love that you tried. Most people wouldn't even care."

Tony *loved* something about her?

He brushed his lips against hers. "You care. It's one of those things that makes you special, Hayden."

"Taylor," she supplied.

"What?" he asked.

"My last name. It's Taylor."

LARISSA WINSTON'S HANDS shook on the steering wheel as she pulled into the parking lot of PharmaTest. But no flashing blue-and-red lights awaited her. No uniformed officers stalked across the front door, ready to take her to jail. Her breath rushed from her chest in an exhaled whoosh. Still, her legs were unsteady as she stepped out of her car and walked to the front door of her office building.

The job had always been so easy. Check the volunteers in, monitor their vitals every hour, and then send them off in the morning with a questionnaire. The last contact she ever had with the test subjects was to cut them a check once they mailed in their completed survey. But last Thursday had changed all that.

Something different must have been in the formula of HB121 because instead of sleeping all night long, four of her patients had not only been fully awake, but they'd also attempted to walk out the door. And they'd been in a partying mood. She'd tried to physically block them from leaving, but then the filmmaker had lifted his camera and asked if she planned to hold them against their will.

She had not been trained to handle this, and she was going to lose her job. You didn't let four subjects stroll out of the lab to wreak havoc and get to keep your job. Even if you did manage to get them to sign waivers. She'd spent the weekend trying to track down two of the four test subject volunteers with no luck at all.

One of the volunteer's cars still waited in the parking lot, which was a horrible sign, right? Larissa raced over to the vehicle to check on the note she'd left under the windshield wiper. It wasn't there. She'd begged for the subject to contact her in that missive, but it had either blown away or was being used as evidence for later.

"Compose yourself," she said aloud, and forced a little calm into her system.

She'd be opening the office in fifteen minutes. At eleven, Dr. Mitch Durant would stop into the office to look over the initial results from Thursday's testing. That flutter of excitement that usually danced in her stomach at the idea of seeing, talking and spending some time alone with the studious research physician didn't materialize.

Now only a tight ball of dread settled heavily in the bottom of her gut. She fought back a wave of nausea. What if her negligence cost him his research? He paid PharmaTest a lot of money to monitor and maintain the integrity of his life's work. She'd never be able to forgive herself if all his research was lost. A true waste of all he'd worked for, but even more importantly, the benefits of HB121 as a medication to be used on those injured in battle or in accidents would be set back possibly years, when countless people could benefit from it *now*. And it was all her fault.

But she still had two hours before the doctor arrived. All weekend long she'd searched the internet and all the social media sites for any hint of her four subjects. It wasn't until this morning that she remembered she had something that might break things open for her— subject thirty-five had left her phone here.

Larissa's heels clapped against the concrete as she raced to the front door and quickly punched in the key code for the knob to unlock. She took five minutes to perform her normal office routine: picking up Saturday's mail from the floor where the carrier had dropped it through the slot, starting a pot of coffee and twisting the rod on the miniblinds to let in a little of the morning sunlight.

But once those tasks were done, her palms started to sweat and her hands shook as she activated PharmaTest's voice mail. Larissa deflated with each call that wasn't test subjects seventy-eight and thirty-five or twelve and ninety-two.

That still left thirty-five's cell phone. As with most people, thirty-five had protected her phone with a password, but had one of those talkie things that could activate the phone book with the lock still in place.

"Call Mom."

Nothing. No response.

"Call Dad."

Still nothing. Poor subject thirty-five.

Then on a long shot she ordered the phone to call Bae. And nothing.

Okay, so that plan didn't work. Her next big idea was to simply wait and see if anyone called thirty-five's phone. Then answer and try to get as much information out of the caller as she could.

Of course in the perfect of most perfect scenarios, the drugs would wear off all four of the subjects and they would go on with their lives. None the wiser. But what were the chances of that? Nil and none.

At nine, two figures passed by her window and Larissa sucked in a deep breath. She'd run through a lot of setups in her mind of how she'd track the patients down and keep them safe, but the scenario of the two of them just dropping in on the office first thing Monday morning hadn't been one of them. She'd never been that lucky in her life.

Of course if those two just kept on walking past her door, she'd be right. But no, they stopped right outside the door and stepped inside. Larissa had never been so grateful or so nervous in her life.

Subjects seventy-eight and thirty-five approached her.

Honestly, even if she'd be going to jail soon, Larissa had never been happier to see two people. She also had no idea how to handle this. She stood and smiled because, when in doubt, always smile.

"Good morning. Would you like some coffee?" And when in doubt, look for a way to escape and prolong the unavoidable.

"Yes," thirty-five said.

"Do you recognize us?" asked seventy-eight. The filmmaker was all business, not to be distracted by dark roast or caffeine.

Larissa nodded and gave up the excuse of fleeing to the break room to prepare their coffee before they talked. "Yes," she said. "Why don't we go into the conference room? We'll be more comfortable there."

PharmaTest rarely received visitors on nontesting days, but she'd still be able to watch the front door and answer the phones if she left the conference room door open and sat at the head of the table.

PT's conference room wasn't large, as the company acted as a middleman between researchers, governmental regulatory officials and pharmaceutical companies. No big deals were hatched between these walls, and usually the space was mostly utilized as a private area to question test subjects. The furnishings were modest with posters of healthy and happy people—all healthy and happy due to modern medicine—gracing the walls. The subject waiting areas were much nicer, with an eye to comfort, relaxation and entertainment while the testers were administered medications and waited out their experiment time.

Larissa pulled their individual files, but she didn't really need to open them. She'd pored over the details they'd provided, even dropping by Ms. Taylor's home several times throughout the weekend to see if she'd returned to her apartment. Thirty-five was a local, but seventy-eight was from out of town—California, if she recalled—but these two appeared very cozy together. Their body language shouted *couple*.

He pulled out the chair for her.

She patted his shoulder.

And then there were the special glances and smiles.

Okay, well good for them. And maybe good for her, too. If they were still in that euphoric, newly enthralled stage of their relationship, they surely wouldn't want anything messy like threatening her job or Mitch's, er, Dr. Durant's research to pop their enraptured love bubble.

Larissa cleared her throat. "Ms. Taylor, I remember from your intake interview that you've participated in several medical and pharmaceutical clinical studies, although this was your first one with us."

"And last," she stated, her voice firm.

Okay, so maybe the love bubble wouldn't be protecting Larissa's job. Well, it was to be expected. She should never have even entertained the idea. Hope was a dangerous thing. "I understand, but I'd like to tell you a little about the drug you were given and just what it will do. It's designed for traumatic emergency situations. Imagine a child hurt in a car crash or a soldier wounded in the field, desperately needing life-saving surgery. The medication can be given orally, which makes it ideal for remote locations and field hospitals. Think about it—no worrying about sterilized needles and IVs, although there should be a version of that ready for trial tests later in the year."

"But we were awake and talking, I'd assume most medications like that would put you to sleep."

Larissa nodded. "Yes, usually when a doctor performs an operation it's ideal for the patient to be unconscious. Obviously they won't panic, their blood pressure won't elevate due to fear and they're immobilized so they can't interfere with the surgeon's work. But for certain kinds of trauma it's better for the patient to be conscious and able to answer questions—brain surgery for one. And on the battlefield there's not the luxury of an operating room. Sometimes you must move the patient, and if they're able to walk, well… I'm sure you can see the benefits of the possibilities afforded by this drug."

"Yes, I can," Ms. Taylor said, her voice not as firm, the anger no longer as palpable. "So that explains the pain relief, but what about the memory loss?"

"That's the most experimental part of this medication. Several peer-reviewed studies show that patients heal faster if they don't have to relive their trauma over and over again in their head. HB121 aids with that."

The filmmaker leaned forward, his broad shoulder gently brushing Ms. Taylor's. Shielding her? Yes, definitely bordering on couple territory. Strange, her life was about to fall apart because of this new medication, while theirs had taken on a whole new facet. She was genuinely happy for them, especially as she'd been hoping for something similar with Dr. Mitch Durant, but that would never be now.

"Why did you let us leave the building?"

"Usually the subjects wait in the patient area or sleep in the room provided. They're quiet. Malleable. But you…" Larissa shook her head, remembering the stress and strain of that night. "You guys were charged. You couldn't wait to get out of here, and when I tried to stop you, Mr. Garcia flipped on his camera phone so I could 'confess to the world' that I was kidnapping you. You did sign a waiver before you left."

The man grimaced and had the grace to look uncomfortable. "That sounds like something I'd say."

"We found some pictures on his phone of us with another couple. They were in the drug study with us, right?"

Larissa nodded. Slowly. This was dangerous ground for another reason: patient confidentiality.

"I can't give too many details because of privacy laws, but let me reassure you that, um, everything is being done for them, as well."

"But you have found them. They're okay?"

She sort of knew where they were. "No need for you to worry." Perfect answer. Leave the panic to Larissa.

Ms. Taylor exhaled and flashed her a grateful smile, which made Larissa feel even worse. *Get them out of here.*

"I have a few additional forms for you to sign, discharging yourself and us from follow-up interviews. And liability." She slipped that last one in quickly, hoping they wouldn't notice. She doubted the forms they'd signed Thursday would hold up in a court of law. And for the icing on the cake, she presented Ms. Taylor with her phone. "You left that here Thursday night."

Ms. Taylor smiled and reached for her phone, then tucked it in her purse without looking at the screen. "Thanks," she mumbled.

Something was wrong here. Clearly the chemistry between them had sizzled Thursday night. They were strangers then, but not now. They'd been so anxious to get their answers, but now neither one seemed to be in any particular hurry to leave. Nor did they blink an eye when she mentioned liability. Which reminded her, she should race to grab those forms before they changed their minds. She might actually be able to keep her job.

"Still interested in that coffee?" she asked.

"Yes, thank you. That would be lovely."

Larissa tried to catch a word of their conversation as the two talked quietly, but she deciphered nothing.

She quickly located the forms, two working fountain pens—so there'd be no delays—and poured a cup of coffee for Ms. Taylor. The expensive kind, just to seal the deal.

"Here we go," she announced cheerfully as she placed the paperwork in front of them and set the mug of steaming java in front of almost-former-subject number thirty-five.

As the two read the forms, Larissa's gaze strayed to the clock. Not bad on the timing. If she could wrap this up in the next fifteen minutes, she'd still have an hour to locate ninety-two and twelve before Dr. Durant arrived. And there fluttered the butterflies at the thought of the sexy doctor.

Since Thursday night, she hadn't felt one glimmer of hope that maybe everything could work out all right. Her stomach lurched, and not the good kind of lurch that the doctor evoked. Was it really going to be this easy? Really? She reminded herself of her earlier warning hope was dangerous.

They both scribbled their names at the bottom of the forms, but instead of gathering their things and leaving, Ms. Taylor sat and savored her coffee while Mr. Garcia sat and savored her when she wasn't noticing.

Then it became clear. They'd got to this point by focusing on solving the mystery of what happened to them. Now, no longer under the effects of HB121 or in doubt of the reasons for their memory loss, what bound them together?

She eyed the clock again. She didn't have time for matchmaking, but then, they weren't suing her. "There's one last effect of the drug. It's rare, but it has shown up occasionally in the trials. Some people refer to the phenomenon as a clarity of thought. Others as a lowering of inhibitions so they could pursue what they really want. I'm glad you two found each other. I wish you both luck."

Tony walked Hayden to her car. That morning she'd repacked the overnight bag she'd brought with her, stowing it in the trunk of her car before they entered PharmaTest.

Lowering of inhibitions so they could pursue what they want.

Had HB121 given him that? The ability to drop the emotional baggage that told him a fine woman like Hayden should never go for him? He wanted her and he'd pursued her. Never leaving her in doubt that he wanted her.

Until now.

Because everything inside him screamed not to let her go. But they'd only discussed their time together as lasting until they learned all the secrets of Thursday night.

Both their steps slowed as they approached her car.

Wait, no. That first night together he'd mentioned two weeks. It was the perfect solution.

She smiled up at him, and like always, all rational thought fled. He became Tarzan—me want. "I had a great time with you, Tony. Probably the best time of my life."

She wrapped her arms around his waist and he drew her slight body to him. Holy hell, he was in trouble, and it wasn't because Hayden stood in the circle of his arms with her head pressed against his chest, and that sex was only the third idea that had seized his brain instead of the first. The first idea was that he could hold Hayden like this forever.

But he didn't come from a forever kind of family.

Short-term all the way. He came from a family of screw-ups and he was no exception. Hayden had her own rough start in things, and didn't need another weight dragging her down when she was just about to fly.

And yet… *Pursue what you want.* "Don't leave me yet," he told her, kissing the tip of her nose.

"I'm not ready for this to end, either," she confessed with a shaky laugh.

He rubbed his chin, but couldn't stop what must be one damn goofy smile from spreading across his face. What the hell was he thinking? He'd documented too many screwed-over-by-love stories to believe in anything like love at first sight, but he'd been falling for Hayden since the moment he'd opened his eyes to find her naked in his bed. "Fallen."

"Fallen?" she asked, confusion knitting her brow.

"That woman at PharmaTest said the drug could give you clarity of thought."

Hayden nodded. "One of the side effects."

He cupped her face, the softness of her cheek a drug in itself. "I can only tell myself you don't fall in love with a person in two days before it starts sounding less like a fact and more like I'm trying to convince myself of something."

"Love?"

"I'm not ready for us to end."

10

TONY FOLLOWED HER in his car to her apartment, but it wasn't to get more of her things. They'd cleared out his hotel room, and the man was moving in. For the next two weeks.

He loved her.

She loved him.

It was crazy. Nuts. It was the very definition of delusional recklessness. The reverse of her usual calm and rational engineering soul. And she just didn't care. He parked beside her in the lot outside her complex, and then the two of them raced hand in hand to her door.

Hayden unlocked it and tugged him inside. He slammed the door shut with his foot, then drew her against his chest. It was like a first kiss because this time there was no fantasy, no secrets—he knew her name and where she lived. His kisses were more passionate now, less controlled and fully demanding.

"I could kiss you all day," she murmured.

Her shirt and her new cool-mint bra landed on the floor while she tore at the buttons on his shirt.

Then she was pressed against him skin to skin, her nipples tightening against the strength of his pecs. She trailed her fingers down the leanness of his six-pack until his belt blocked her forward progress.

"Where's the bedroom?"

"Behind you. The door on the left." Then he swooped her up in his arms and carried her to bed. He followed her to the mattress and made love to her until their bodies were exhausted.

"I was afraid I'd never see you again after we talked to the lady at PharmaTest," she revealed later as they snuggled under the covers of her bed.

"But now we have two weeks to pursue what we want."

Two weeks. Her last thoughts before she drifted into a deep and sated sleep was that she wouldn't worry about how short that seemed; she'd only work to make their time together perfect.

On Wednesday, semester grades were posted and Hastings Engineering made her a formal offer of employment. She asked for a start date after Tony returned to California and they agreed. She'd need work then to keep her mind off the fact that the love of her life was moving on, and to remind her what real life was all about.

"I'm really proud of you, Hayden," he told her after she showed him the contract. "You worked harder than anyone to get your degree, but you knew what you wanted and went after it."

She *had* worked hard, but it was strangely easy to forget all about engineering and throw herself into helping Tony. Over the next few days they fell into an easy pattern of working together on his cowboy documentary. By day they'd talk and laugh as they drove out to the remote locations where the cowboys worked. He'd film and she'd interview these rugged men and women, sometimes even camping along the trail with their subjects, listening to stories around the campfire. She'd even grown fond of cowboy poetry.

When Tony needed to change creative focus, he'd ask her questions for his next project about drug testing, and she'd describe her experiences volunteering for various medical trials. He was incredible at multitasking, going from one subject to the next, even tossing out suggestions for two more documentaries down the road.

His multitasking abilities also definitely extended to the bedroom. Or backseat of the car on a lonely stretch of rural Texas road. Or on a bedroll under a blanket of stars after the cowhands went to sleep. Still, she was happy to be home again now and to have Tony all to herself.

"Are you blushing?" Tony asked her.

She rubbed the back of her neck and avoided his gaze. What the heck was wrong with her? She liked having sex with this man. Loved it. Why should she even be remotely embarrassed at being caught thinking about making love with him? Just because she'd grown up with an outdated outlook on sex didn't mean she had to suffer with it forever. Hadn't she overcome that already?

She met his gaze, allowed her eyes to briefly fall to his lips, then rise back up again to meet his. "Not blushing. Flushed. I was thinking about you."

Awareness flared in his eyes and he swallowed.

"Sex hasn't been on my mind so much since that picture study I did."

"Picture study?"

"Well, it wasn't actually a drug trial. I was stuck in an MRI machine that scanned my brain as they showed me pictures of, well let's just call it 'sexy times.' I rated the pictures on a turn-on scale of one to five and the tester would see if the activity in my brain verified what I said."

"You were looking at sexy pictures and asked which ones turned you on? Yeah, no way I'd be interested in that," he teased.

"That's not all. There'd be videos and we'd also rate the suggestions the actors gave to their partners."

"Like what?"

"Well, taking your finger in my mouth and demanding you think of me whenever you use it was one of the sexy ideas I was asked to respond to."

"Something that still drives me crazy, by the way."

"Guess I should have rated it higher than a four."

"I almost dread what you said was a five."

"C'mon, I'll show you." She grabbed his hand and led him into the kitchen. "So the suggestion for this room was to look at your man and ask, 'Do you think the floor would be too cold for sex?'"

"Mmmmm, I'm willing to give it a try."

"So I guess you'd rate that one as fiveworthy."

"Definitely," he assured her.

"Okay, follow me—I have another place for us to try." And she led him into the bathroom. "The idea here is for me to light a few candles, and then wonder aloud, 'Could we both fit in this tub to make love?'"

"That would do it."

"I'm beginning to think you're easy."

Tony laughed. "Beginning? Give me another."

"Next I write words on your body, and you have to guess what I'm spelling."

He reached for the button on his jeans. "Let's try it."

"You don't have to take off your pants. Your stomach will do." But the joke was on her when he lifted his shirt up and over his head and tossed it on top of the hamper. Her mouth dried. Would there ever be a time when his chest and roped abs didn't turn her on?

She flattened her palm against the hardness of his chest.

"Spell, woman, and I take points off for penmanship."

With a smothered laugh she began to write. Her fingertip grew sensitive as she stroked the heat of his skin. The muscles of his stomach contracted and tightened as she wrote. She forgot about form and only concentrated on sensation. His hand captured hers, stilling her progress. His breath teased her temple. "Whenever you write something, I want you to think about this moment," he whispered into her ear. "How you made a man hungry. I want you, Hayden. Now." His lips lowered to her mouth, but she pulled away.

"You have to guess what I wrote."

"Tell me," he urged, his voice so sexy and filled with need her legs began to shake.

"I wrote, 'Where would you like me to touch you right now?'"

"Everywhere," he said, then wrapped her in his arms and drew her into the bedroom.

NOW THAT THEY were back in Dallas, she was determined to show him the city. They explored the downtown and the surrounding areas on elaborate dates that took her breath away. He even took her back to Lavish so they could swing from the chandelier, the cage and the bed. At night they made love until they couldn't keep their eyes open.

"Since we don't remember our first night together, I'm guaranteeing you won't forget another one."

It was a challenge to himself and a promise to her that she adored.

Te adoro.

She adored the man. How was she going to let him go?

The Friday before she began work, Hayden couldn't put it off anymore—she had to shop. Jeans and T-shirts and hoodies filled her closet, but she needed business attire. At least a week's worth, then after her first paycheck she could indulge a little more.

She came home with her arms full of bags, and she imagined doing a fashion show for Tony with all the stuff she'd bought, but when she keyed into her apartment, he was talking excitedly on his phone. He flashed her a thumbs-up sign, so she carried her new clothes into the bedroom, taking them out of the sacks and hanging them in the closet.

Suddenly Tony gripped her around the waist and spun her around. "I've just gotten the funding for a new documentary. A companion to *Lost Causes* but it would focus on the plight of girls on the streets."

She hugged him tight. "Oh, Tony, I'm so happy for you."

"The best part is, if I can pack the car up tonight, I could be back in LA by Sunday and start on it ASAP."

Leaving her was the best part? Her arms flopped to her sides. "But you still have two more days in Texas."

"I've finished all the principle photography here. All that's left is the editing, which I can do at home."

"Home? I thought you were beginning to think of this place as your home. With me."

He rubbed his chin and backed away. "Now's not the time to discuss this."

Avoidance. Their old standby. "Well, when is?" she asked, propping her hands on her hips. "You're leaving in a few hours."

"You knew we had only the two weeks," he said, his body growing rigid.

"Two weeks *together*, sure, but not two weeks *only*. I figured when the time came we'd discuss how we'd make a long-distance relationship work."

He took another step away from her. "I don't do relationships."

"You don't *do*?" she asked, exaggerating the last word and feeling like a shrew. "I thought we were building something together."

"I apologize. I never meant to give you that impression," he told her, his voice cool and his manner so formal.

Her shoulders slumped as she mentally reviewed every conversation they'd ever had about the future and realized those equaled one big zero. "No, you never misled me. I presumed too much."

The tension in his shoulders visibly lessoned. "I tried to make the time we had perfect."

Something in his words triggered the part of her brain she'd been ignoring for the past two weeks. The cautionary part that always put a damper on the fun to spout off boring warnings and suggestions like *slow down* or *maybe give this a second thought*.

"You tried to make it perfect?" she asked. As she mentally turned over every moment, yes, since he'd moved into her apartment with her, their time together had been nothing but perfection. He'd planned these over-the-top, romantic dates that would put a bachelor-dating TV show to shame. They spent evenings exploring *her* favorite things and *her* interests and their nights making love.

He'd invited her along to the film sites, and she'd assumed he'd wanted to share that part of his life with her. To include her in what had taken him off the streets and saved his life. But now she realized he'd taken her with him because she'd asked. Hell, this was the closest they'd ever come to an argument.

Hayden rubbed at the tension forming in her temples. "So was any of this real?"

"What do you mean? Of course it was real."

"At least be honest with yourself. You didn't try to make these two weeks perfect for me. You wanted perfection."

"What's wrong with that? We should all strive to be the best. To get the best out of ourselves and the people around us."

She nodded. "Yes, it's what we should want, but with the understanding that it's not what we're going to get. Perfection isn't real. It's an illusion. For a guy who's usually pretty in touch with what's going on in his own head, you're missing out on a lot of things."

"Oh? Enlighten me."

"You're a filmmaker, you work to make everything in your movie flawless."

"Documentarian. I don't make features. Believe me, I know and show the way the world is."

"So that you can make it better. It's one of the reasons I love you. Anyone could have filmed those kids in *Lost Causes*, but not everyone would have worked to get the funding and the support to give those guys a shot at something better. Or would have gone back year after year to challenge and encourage them."

"It's my job."

"And you performed that same routine on me, too."

"How so?"

"That whole trip from the roller rink to the cabin, those were all my fantasies. I've wanted a car painted like a ladybug since I was nine. Boom—you made it happen. I've never gambled, you take me to a casino. I've never been to Oklahoma, so we go on a road trip. It's so clear now. Somehow you think the only way a woman will love you is to be perfect and give her whatever she wants and to fix whatever's wrong for her. You were so intent on convincing me that you were a good guy, but you never convinced yourself." Something he'd probably internalized as a little boy raised by a woman incapable of actually giving love.

"Did you squeeze in some pop psychology classes in between those engineering labs?" he asked. Then he stomped into the spare bedroom where he'd set up his editing equipment. Without a word, he began backing up his files and shutting everything down.

She leaned against the door frame. "But I fell under the spell of having you give and give and give to me, and it was wrong."

"You're rejecting me now?" he asked as he wound a power cord around his arm so it would pack neatly.

"No. Never, but I know me, too. I like to fix my own problems, not have someone do it for me."

Lay it out for him now. Show him all your cards.

She stilled his hands with hers, drawing his attention. "You, Anthony Garcia, having *you* in my life makes it better. To come home to you. To share the quiet times with you. We've worked so hard to keep up the adventure that drew us together we forgot to keep it real. I want us to work, but I also need something I can trust."

The light behind his dark eyes faded, and his face lost all expression. She'd just broken the spell.

"You don't trust me?" Disbelief and anger and anguish laced every word of his question.

All his life Tony had been labeled as untrustworthy. From his mother to the school to the judicial system.

He'd fought himself and the opinions of others to become a man who could be counted on. Trusted.

Hayden battled every instinct that screamed at her to apologize. To reassure him that she didn't mean what she'd said and had only spoken in anger, because only some of that was true. She did trust him. With her life and her body. No, it was him that couldn't trust in his own potential.

"You say you love me, then at least fight for what's growing between us. You can *do* a relationship, even a long-distance one. We can text and call and video chat. Scores of other couples manage it."

"Don't you see, Hayden? I don't want to fight. I've had enough of that to last two lifetimes." He grabbed his computer and his suitcase and headed for the door.

"You film reality, Tony, but you don't want to live it."

He pressed his lips together, and for one brief moment she thought maybe he'd give her a reaction. Something. Instead he reached out and gently touched her hair. Saying goodbye. "These have been the most amazing weeks of my life. I hope you won't look back and have…regrets."

He kissed the tip of her nose as he always did, then spun away from her and left her apartment.

WHAT HAPPENED WHEN you put all your cards on the table and lost?

She had to start looking for some better metaphors, because all these poker references reminded her too much of the man who'd dumped her.

Hayden had done the ice-cream bender.

The movie binge.

The vows to permanently go off men and get a couple of rescue dogs.

Okay, the dog plan was a go. With her new salary at Hastings Engineering she could afford the rent on a small two-bedroom home with a yard. Great for a puppy or two to run around in and play fetch. At night they could snuggle on the couch and watch movies and take walks after work. Sounded perfect—nope, scratch that because nothing was the *P* word—as she'd childishly begun to think of it. Instead the plan sounded really good. Workable. Doable.

She'd even driven out to PharmaTest to see if being at the place where they'd first met could somehow break the lonely spell, but Larissa no longer worked there and Hayden had left quickly, feeling stupid.

She'd settled into that transitional phase of life. No longer a student, she now embraced full-fledged tax-paying, retirement-planning adulthood. So when she wasn't packing up her apartment for her impending move, or wasn't driving around in the neighborhoods surrounding her new place of work for rental properties, Hayden searched the internet for the average length of time it took for a broken heart to heal. General consensus seemed to be about three months.

She looked up advice on how to speed up that three months, but the best advice was to stop doing things you used to do together. So basically that knocked out driving, sleeping and eating. One article suggested listing all the qualities that made up an ideal mate, then comparing and contrasting those to the last guy. Surely an exercise that demonstrated just how far from perfect—ugh, she hated the word and there it was again—the ex really was. But five minutes later she'd tossed that magazine aside because Tony's qualities were her match for the ideal mate. Except for the running away, the avoidance and shying away from intense emotion.

When the third month of her getting-over-Tony plan neared, she tried to focus on enjoying the calm of aloneness for a while. Only her coworkers seemed obsessed with talking about their partners and asking about Hayden's social life. Significant othering was definitely part of the adult world.

Except for Tony's adult world.

He was apparently happy just where he was, moving from one brief relationship to another. Oh, and why wouldn't he be happy? He'd escaped his past and built a great present for himself.

For the first time it crossed Hayden's mind that he'd worked so hard to escape the devastation of his past and succeeded, only for her to tell him that because he didn't want to move forward with her, there was something wrong with him. She wrapped her arms around herself and realized she had treated him terribly. Unfairly.

He'd hoped she'd not look back on their time together with regret. Well, she had tons of regret now, mostly that she'd added to the conflict in his life. Hadn't she expected him to bend to her version of love?

THREE DAYS LATER, she came home to find a package waiting on her doorstep, forwarded from her old address. When she spotted Tony's name on the return address her heartbeat sped up as adrenaline rushed through her. The puppies barked in greeting when she opened the door and she followed them outside to the backyard, hugging the parcel to her chest. She tore off the packaging as the dogs frolicked and tumbled around her feet. A piece of cardboard dropped to the grass and Boots shredded it with her paws and teeth. Hayden smiled a moment at their antics, then looked at the gift Tony had mailed her.

A DVD fell into her hand. He'd finished the cowboy movie.

He'd tucked a note inside the case. "I wanted you to be the first to see it."

"Who wants a treat?" she called to the puppies, and they raced to beat her to the back door.

After preparing their favorite snack of peanut butter, she popped the DVD into the player and pressed Play.

The beautiful Texas horizon filled her TV screen. She'd kissed and loved with Tony as he'd filmed dozens of sunsets, and she remembered the warmth of the fading autumn sun and the searing heat of his kisses. Then the screen faded to black and words appeared.

Dedicated, with love to Hayden.

With love? What did that mean? Did Tony still love her?

No, she wasn't going to analyze his words. Hayden only wanted to enjoy the power of his work. She sat enthralled for the next hour and a half as the beautiful story Tony wove together of the lonely and harsh life of a modern-day cowboy came to life.

He ended the film with one of the shots she'd

suggested—a lone rider on the flat plains of a drought-ridden Texas. The camera widened its shot, taking in the rugged stretch of the wildness surrounding the rider until he was lost in the expanse. Then it faded to black and the credits rolled to the sound of the wind on the Texas plains rather than music. It was haunting and natural and beautiful, and Hayden loved Tony even more. She ached with her need for him.

Damn, those three months would have to start all over again now.

Tony had loved her. He had. Just not enough.

Hayden closed her eyes and allowed the wrenching pain to course through her, living each wave of aching hurt. She fell asleep on the couch, only waking when the puppies rang their bell to go outside.

THE MUSIC BLASTED from Tony's stereo as he drove along the Pacific coastline, the waves and surf right outside his window. And he was miserable. Each day a little more than the one before.

He wasn't prepared to admit Hayden was right about all her assertions. On some points, she'd nailed him. He'd wanted to keep the adventure going between them because he was so damn in love with her. He couldn't understand how he could keep such a woman around if he didn't make every night something to look forward to.

He'd abandoned his work on the drug-testing documentary. Every time he picked up his notes he thought about her. When he planned a shooting schedule, he'd remember her smile and a wave of pure loneliness bashed him in the gut. And damn if he wasn't still trying to forget her suggestion to think of her every time he used his finger. Which was constantly.

He couldn't work. He couldn't eat. He couldn't sleep. Tony had to do something or he'd lose his mind. He hated the way things had ended between them, primarily because he knew Hayden had been right. He was a coward, a man who used his past as a shield so he wouldn't have to struggle to make things work.

What an idiot. He'd already lost the best thing that had ever happened to him.

He'd got soft. But not so soft he didn't remember how to change his life. She'd accused him of not being willing to fight, but that was changing. Now. He clicked on his phone. "Route me to Dallas, Texas."

THREE MONTHS TO the day of when Tony had walked out of her life, a Los Angeles area code popped up on Hayden's cell screen. She'd deleted his contact, but she'd somehow managed to memorize his number.

Why would he call now? She'd finally managed to put away the ice cream and the streaming service.

Her finger hovered over the Send Call to Voice Mail button. But she couldn't really accuse a man of not facing reality when she played the avoidance game.

"Hello?"

"There's a family of four living in your old apartment."

Hayden almost choked. "You're here? In Dallas?" she managed to ask between coughs.

"I came for you."

A shudder racked her body. Not I came to see you, but I came *for* you. Better tack on another three months.

"Hayden, are you going to give me your address? I've done nothing but drive for two days and I need to see you."

She quickly recited her street number and hung up. Hayden needed time to compose herself, and if he was at her old apartment, it would take him less than ten minutes to get to her new place. Boots and Harley each got a peanut butter treat and she let them out in the backyard so nothing would disturb their conversation.

I've done nothing but drive.

Did that mean he'd just aimed his car toward Texas on the spur of the moment? Hayden wouldn't doubt it; he loved the big, romantic gestures. She placed a few dishes in the sink, and then raced to make up her bed. Tony preferred neatness.

Wait a minute. This was her home and he was the one who'd dumped her. The bed he could see as it was— messy. But not her hair.

She popped into the bathroom and ran a brush through her hair and wiped off a smudge of dirt one of the puppies had gifted on her cheek.

Barking announced Tony's arrival before the doorbell. The dogs were outside and still knew when a stranger was at the door. She eyed him through the peephole. Tony waited on her stoop, looking tired and worn and gorgeous as hell. Had he come for her, really?

Hayden squeezed her eyes tight, and damn if a tear still didn't slip from the corner of her eye in some cliché form of torture. She did not want to cry in front

of him. But then, why the hell not? They'd done the su-
perficial thing. This was real life, and if she wanted to
have a grown-up relationship with the man in front of
her, he had to participate when things weren't made up
of great shots, perfect sunsets and shallow emotions.
She opened the door.

"You broke my heart when you left," she told him.
No anger. No accusations. Just simple truth. That was
not how she'd wanted to start this conversation. It
sounded too accusatory, especially when she'd practi-
cally shouted at him that he didn't know how to love
the right way.

Tony blanched. "Don't say that," he urged.

Okay, now she was angry. "Why not? Because then
you'd have to acknowledge that it hurt when you left?
That I have feelings? That you have feelings?"

"Hayden, please understand. I don't think I've ever
looked in my mother's eyes without seeing disappointment. I left you because I had to. Because one day I'm
sure you're going to look at me and wonder, what the
hell am I doing with this loser? The idea that you could
look at me like that, rips my gut out."

She shook her head. "Tony, how can you even con-
sider yourself as a loser? After all you've accomplished.
You're smart and funny and against almost all the odds
imaginable, you are rising in a field that must be tough
as hell—and with no help, nothing from your family.
You're amazing."

"Doesn't make me a good guy."

And there it was. "You don't believe you're a good
person, do you?"

Tony's gaze dropped from hers.

"The fact that you're worried whether or not you're a nice guy answers that question. You're the man who turned his back at the cabin when I was naked. You're the one who waited to kiss me until I was ready. Not only did you stick with me every step of the way, you made what could have been horrible and scary, fun and adventurous."

He met her eyes then, and she stole a step toward him.

"And as for the disappointment you saw in your mom's eyes, that was her issue. Not yours. You were a child. I'm angry all over again at her for saddling you with that stupid doubt about yourself. Are you going to say things that will irritate the crap out of me? Yes. But you..." She reached for his hand. "As long as you love me, you will never disappoint me."

"If I lose you—the real me, that is, not make-everything-perfect guy. Me. If I lose you..."

"You left me to go back to California, and I still love you. I can't even remember wish-fulfillment Tony. It's you, Anthony Garcia, who was there beside me every step of the way."

His hands fisted at his sides. Then he reached for her, hugged her tight. "I will love you forever," he said over and over again as he stroked her hair and down her back.

Hayden sucked in a breath that came out as a sob.

"*Cariño*, I didn't come here to make you cry. I came to give you this," and he brought something forward from behind his back.

She hadn't even realized he'd been hiding something. Then her jaw dropped. "Is that a... Is that a mop?"

He grinned. *"Si."*

Had he just used the Spanish on her because he knew she had a weakness for it? She shook her head. "I know it's a mop—I mean why?"

"Because I want to live a real life with you, Hayden. I want to mop the floors, and take out the trash with you. And later we can balance my checkbook. But if you're lucky we can do yours next," he promised, his voice low and seductive.

She sucked in a deep breath, and his warm strength surrounded her. Oh, how she'd missed him. His carnal scent, the urgency of his kisses.

"Now, ordinarily, if I wanted to ask someone to share her life with me, I'd order up a hot air balloon or send you on a treasure hunt, but that's not me anymore. What did you call that version of me?"

"Wish-fulfillment Tony," she admitted.

"No grand gestures. This is just you. And me. Telling you I want to call you mine. Forever."

Now that was perfect. She flung herself into his arms, and his lips came down on hers.

After a few moments, his fingers curved around her shoulder and he gently held her away from him. "It's not going to be easy. I travel around the country most of the year. Long-distance relationships are tough."

"I think I can come up with a few ways to keep us close despite the distance," she assured him. "Believe it or not, I've actually experimented with a little filming for my boyfriend. The sexy kind," she added in a thick Texas drawl and a wink.

"Which, if I remember correctly, he didn't get to keep. Will that be different now?"

"I may have investigated some encryption technology."

"Then I may have one big gesture up my sleeve." He shoved his hand up his arm, pushing back his jacket.

"Oh, you mean you literally have something up your sleeve."

"I got this about three weeks ago."

On his skin stretched a perfect likeness of her dragon tattoo.

"They're not a perfect pair. But they are a matching set."

"I couldn't agree more."

* * * * *

REQUEST YOUR FREE BOOKS!
2 FREE NOVELS PLUS 2 FREE GIFTS!

Ⓗ HARLEQUIN®

Blaze

red-hot reads!

YES! Please send me 2 FREE Harlequin® Blaze® novels and my 2 FREE gifts (gifts are worth about $10). After receiving them, if I don't wish to receive any more books, I can return the shipping statement marked "cancel." If I don't cancel, I will receive 4 brand-new novels every month and be billed just $4.74 per book in the U.S. or $5.21 per book in Canada. That's a savings of at least 14% off the cover price. It's quite a bargain. Shipping and handling is just 50¢ per book in the U.S. and 75¢ per book in Canada.* I understand that accepting the 2 free books and gifts places me under no obligation to buy anything. I can always return a shipment and cancel at any time. Even if I never buy another book, the two free books and gifts are mine to keep forever.

150/350 HDN GH2D

Name _____ (PLEASE PRINT)

Address _____ Apt. #

City _____ State/Prov. _____ Zip/Postal Code

Signature (if under 18, a parent or guardian must sign)

Mail to the **Reader Service:**
IN U.S.A.: P.O. Box 1867, Buffalo, NY 14240-1867
IN CANADA: P.O. Box 609, Fort Erie, Ontario L2A 5X3

Want to try two free books from another line?
Call 1-800-873-8635 or visit www.ReaderService.com.

* Terms and prices subject to change without notice. Prices do not include applicable taxes. Sales tax applicable in N.Y. Canadian residents will be charged applicable taxes. Offer not valid in Quebec. This offer is limited to one order per household. Not valid for current subscribers to Harlequin Blaze books. All orders subject to credit approval. Credit or debit balances in a customer's account(s) may be offset by any other outstanding balance owed by or to the customer. Please allow 4 to 6 weeks for delivery. Offer available while quantities last.

Your Privacy—The Reader Service is committed to protecting your privacy. Our Privacy Policy is available online at www.ReaderService.com or upon request from the Reader Service.

We make a portion of our mailing list available to reputable third parties that offer products we believe may interest you. If you prefer that we not exchange your name with third parties, or if you wish to clarify or modify your communication preferences, please visit us at www.ReaderService.com/consumerschoice or write to us at Reader Service Preference Service, P.O. Box 9062, Buffalo, NY 14240-9062. Include your complete name and address.

HBI5